The Wine of Astonishment

Stories by Mary Overton

Mary Overton (signature)

La Questa
PRESS

Woodside, California

Cover and text design by Kajun Graphics
Cover illustration by Susan Marie Dopp

ISBN 0-9644348-1-4

Library of Congress Catalog Card Number: 97-65055

Grateful acknowledgement is made to the following publications to reprint
previously published stories:

"Butterfly Girl": *Wellspring*; "Mother Machine": *The Belletrist Review*;
"Ladies in the Trees" was published in another version as "The Encyclopaedia
Salesman": *Wordwrights!*; "After the Kill": *The Southern Anthology*;
"Fly-by-Night Weddings": *Giltedge, New Series*;
"Ruth": *Lansing Citylimits*; "Visiting the Pakistanis": *Potomac Review*;
"After Life" and "Letters to Ellen": *Glimmer Train Stories*;
"The Close": *Treasure House*.

To Matthew Beall, who has a few stories of his own

✤✤✤

Thank you, Corrina Beall,
for your patience, humor, and trust.
Thank you Lou Ann Lacny, Peggy Lewis,
Kim Price-Muñoz,
Julie Schoeberlein, and Marg Wildermann,
for sharing work and laughter.
Thank you, Kate Abbe, e-mail companion,
for your dedication,
your insight, and your friendship.
Thank you, Richard Peabody,
teacher and mentor,
for giving me permission to have
faith in myself.

Contents

Butterfly Girl

MELISSA'S SECRET began when she was three. Her mother tried one day to comfort her. There had been a quarrel between Melissa and her older sister.

"You're just a baby," Mama said, rubbing a dry hand over Melissa's face. "It's hard being a baby."

Melissa nodded.

"When you grow up, it will be different," Mama said. "When you grow up, you can be anything you want to be."

Melissa looked vaguely around the room.

"Listen to me when I'm talking."

Melissa was looking for what she might be.

"You have to work hard," Mama said, "but you can be something special. You can be anything you want to be."

She would like to be her mama's breasts, Melissa thought, soft cups turned upside down.

"Sweetie, don't pull on me there. It's not nice." Mama pried Melissa's fingers from her sweater. Melissa began to scream.

"Stop it. There's nothing wrong with you."

She screamed more, the way she did at night when dark air from the attic leaked into her room. Illuminated by the night light, the dark air floated like smoke from her mama's cigarette. It came from the black hole in the ceiling of her closet. Mama closed the closet door, stuffed towels under it, but the black air got through.

"Outside. Now," Mama said. "I won't listen to this."

Melissa was put in the fenced backyard. She hung forlornly at the gate, watching her big sister Darbie ride a bicycle with training wheels up and down the front walk.

"Crybaby," Darbie taunted and stuck out her tongue.

Melissa walked around the yard then, trying to find something to be when she grew up. It seemed a dangerous and urgent task that must be done immediately. Her heart was heavy with responsibility. Melissa looked at the summer marigolds, at the warped place in the bottom of the chain link fence, at a spider walking on the woodpile, at the pebbly cement platform that held the clothes pole in the ground. She thought about being each of these things.

Melissa crawled into her secret place beneath the overgrown shrubbery. She lay still, cloudy with anxiety, imagining that she was the cool, dusty dirt, complicated with little pieces of pine needles and twigs, shredded dead leaves and round stones.

A butterfly lit in the branch above her. Its wings were heart shaped and copper colored. They folded together like the paper fans Darbie made in Sunday school.

I want to be a butterfly, Melissa thought.

The butterfly basked, open winged, in the sun. Its narrow body and pen-stroke legs held utterly, rigidly still.

"I want to be a butterfly," Melissa said.

The creature leaped into space, unthinking, as if pulled by a string. Three more sailed over Melissa's yard, over her secret place, and together the four butterflies pinwheeled through the air. Their wings were as stiff and thin as copper wire.

Melissa burst after them. "I want to be a butterfly!" she yelled, filled with the joy of a right vision. She ran beneath the fluttery cloud, and the butterflies were courtly. They stayed within her fenced yard. Melissa ran and ran and ran. She ran on her toes, her arms stretched skyward, her face skyward, working hard, practicing to be a butterfly, because her mama and her daddy believed in hard work and Melissa understood without knowing it, that she must work to be the thing she had now decided to be.

For days Melissa practiced running and then for years, until she outran all the children, even the older ones like Darbie. People said she ran with wings on her feet. Whenever Melissa saw a butterfly, and there were more of them back when she was a child, she felt a thrill of kinship.

At last Melissa forgot about becoming a butterfly. She never gave it up. She simply forgot because time went by and it didn't happen and she was getting to an age where she would have to understand certain things. Rather than that, she simply forgot. She forgot the secret place in the shrubbery and the black air seeping through her closet door.

When Melissa was nine her family's fortunes declined.

They moved, and she went to a new school built next to a vacant field. There were no trees or shrubs at her school, only a concrete breezeway where the wind came through fast and mean, and a bare macadam play yard, and beyond that, where it was forbidden to go, the hot field tall with milkweed.

Her new teacher was predatory, like a majestic but heartless hunting bird. When a rowdy boy angered her, the teacher pulled his ear, something Melissa had never seen. The teacher took student papers in a seemingly arbitrary way, held them up and ridiculed them. She had trained the class to laugh. The first time it happened, Melissa was stunned with terror. Her body became too heavy even for her lungs to open, and she could not breathe.

"Just work hard and mind your own business and you'll be fine," Mama said when Melissa came home and dissolved into hysterics.

"You are so feeble," Darbie said.

Melissa continued to cry until she made herself sick. She threw up and developed a fever. The next day she acted so weak and pitiful that Mama kept her home from school.

"What am I going to do with you, a big girl like you?" Mama asked rhetorically as she unpacked kitchen things from a cardboard carton. Wadded newspaper lay in heaps on the floor.

Melissa ate canned chicken-and-rice soup that her mama had heated on the stove. The question of what to do with herself was mysterious. It always involved hard work and, more recently, being smart. It did not yet occur to Melissa to ask if her mama and her daddy had worked hard and if they had gotten what they wanted, this cheap third floor garden apartment next to a railroad track, weary evenings full of TV, one daughter who was scornful and another who needed something done with her.

"We'll get you moved to another class," Mama said. "I'll tell the principal you have a nervous problem. There's always a way to handle these things."

Mama had to go to work, she said, "so you have to go back to school if you want it or not." After lunch the two of them walked through canyons of apartment buildings, crossed the boulevard, entered the breezeway. The journey was still new and perilous, and Melissa wanted to hold Mama's hand.

"A big girl like you," Mama said again, indulgently. "You are an intelligent girl, but not sensible. Daddy and I have always tried to impress upon you girls the importance of using your brains to get what you want." Mama talked the entire way.

✿✿✿

Twenty years later Melissa tried to reconstruct what happened. Her memory and her mother's memory diverged.

"It was the two of us together when we saw the field," Melissa said. She was back home because her daddy was in the hospital with a mild stroke. Now he'd gotten better. Mama and she were able to leave his bedside, get some sleep, but first they talked. They sat on Mama's screened porch and talked, exhausted, about Darbie's several marriages, then about the near financial ruin that had caused them to move so long ago to the apartment, then about the monarch migration.

"Oh, no," Mama said. "It was days later. It was a month later. I never promised I would change your class. There may have been only one fourth grade teacher anyway. It was a small school. And the principal didn't like me. He didn't like anyone from the apartments."

That must be right, Melissa thought, because she remembered a moist, burdensome dread filling her, filling every vessel in her body, like a levee of packed, wet sand. She must have returned to the predatory teacher's class, but she did not remember it, not one second more of being in that room. Her mother insisted there was at least a month more because the butterfly migration did not happen when the family first came to the apartment.

"The monarchs didn't come until we'd been there at least a month," Mama said. "The TV cameras came, I remember. After you were in school that morning, before I went to work, I walked across the boulevard and I watched the TV people filming it."

Melissa was drinking a wine cooler so sweet it stuck to her teeth. She never drank coolers in her own home, but Mama liked them and kept them in the refrigerator. Melissa remembered holding her mama's dry hand, a big girl like her, and looking across the burning field. Holding that hand remained a distinct part of her memory, but Mama said it couldn't be, that Melissa was with her classmates, that all the children came out on the bare macadam to see the miracle of nature.

The field burned.

Afterward, Mama and Daddy took her out of school for a month. It was a calm, quiet time spent with the retired lady next door, Mrs. Clark. They read Reader's Digest condensed books and listened to the radio, and Mrs. Clark taught Melissa a double solitaire card game. Melissa took naps a lot.

The field burned with a humming sound. It was like being God and hearing the murmur of all the world's children praying at bedtime, the cloying urgency of all that longing. Fire flickered up the stalks of milkweed. Copper and black ash floated in the air. The flames beat like shuttering wings. They were wings, a thousand, a hundred thousand monarch wings vibrating over the milkweed. The press of butterfly bodies was unbearable.

Melissa remembered it exactly that way, the press of bodies.

Maybe, her mama said, she was remembering the press of child bodies out on the play yard. The entire school came out to see the butterfly migration. It was something that happened every year in late September. The children were slightly bored even while they relished the time out of class.

Melissa remembered differently. She remembered letting go of Mama's hand. She remembered the unthinking way she ran, frantic, possessed, into the field where it was forbidden to go. She ran into the yielding cushion of butterfly bodies, into the powder of their wide wings.

"Take me with you," she cried.

Melissa put her hands out to them. Utterly trusting, believing, she flew among them, her body changing, her heart squeezed into a tiny black shell of a thorax.

"Take me with you."

After the Kill

My brother bagged his first deer out of season, a doe full of milk. Dougie figured the reason it didn't count against him was because he'd had to kill her with a sledgehammer. This happened the summer of the rabies scare, when my brother turned nineteen and first lived on his own, in the days when he still thought of himself as a hero. My husband, who'd never liked Dougie, said it was proof of my brother's dangerous character, that 999 people out of a thousand could not bash in the skull of a wounded deer.

Dougie called me at five-thirty on a July morning to ask me to bring a camera and film. I had neither, and I did not appreciate the call. My husband and I were doing janitorial and housecleaning work then. We didn't get up until nine.

"Is he drunk?" my husband asked.

"He's had a few beers," I said. "Mostly he's excited."

A few beers at five-thirty in the morning was understandable. Dougie got off his job at four-thirty. He worked a split shift at the Post Office distribution center, doing some kind of menial labor throwing packages from one bin to another. He wanted to be what back then was called a mailman, but we all had our doubts about him making it.

The story Dougie told me over the phone was that the car in front of him surprised a deer in its headlights, hit her, and kept going. Dougie stopped. Thinking quickly, he grabbed the sledge-hammer from among the tools littering the trunk of his car, and he popped the animal right between her ears. Dougie said he looked both ways, stashed the deer in the back seat, and headed home to what my husband unkindly called the Juice Pad.

"Her legs were broken and such," Dougie said. "She was gonna die, so why not grab some meat?"

"You going to butcher her?" I asked.

"Sure."

"Let the meat locker do it," I said. "It's a mess."

"Not this time of year, not in the summer," Dougie said conspiratorially. "They might turn me in to the game warden."

My brother had saved two years of hunting magazines for the articles on "Cleaning Your Kill." The past couple of winters he'd gone hunting with his drunk buddies, but all they'd spotted were deer tracks and turds.

I hung up the phone, and my husband asked in his most cranky voice, "Are you going to go see his deer?"

Joe was up and out of bed already, pulling on his pants like this was a major world crisis. I am married to one of those exasperating people who swears he can not go back to sleep after he's been awakened. Then he blames whatever it is that's wakened him.

"If I can figure out a way so the Pearsalls don't see me," I said.

"Why do you care if they see you?" my husband demanded. "You ought to fire them anyway. You don't make any money there."

"I know."

Joe talked about our housecleaning customers like he owned them, like he was a gift they better appreciate. I was not nearly so pragmatic. We always gave people a list of the things in their house that would be cleaned biweekly. Joe cleaned houses too, in the middle of the day, but he charged extra for any little thing added to the list.

My customers got away with murder. The Pearsalls were the worst, because old Mrs. Pearsall just didn't understand. She thought I was an old-fashioned, four-hour cleaning lady. I could have done the chores on my list in half that time, but every two weeks I gave her a full four hours and did strange jobs like iron patched sheets and scrub bird baths and reorganize forty-two rolls of toilet paper stockpiled in her closet.

Coincidence happens regularly when you are self-employed, but none was more surprising than the call from Bertha Pearsall, who inquired about my ad for housecleaning services. Bertha was old Mrs. Pearsall's daughter and no youngster herself. She'd recently taken early retirement from a government job. All her adult life Bertha had lived with her widowed mother. An interesting twist was that she'd spent her childhood with her father. Mr. and Mrs. Pearsall separated early in their marriage but, in the manner of those days, did not divorce.

I collected crumbs of insight like this in lieu of the better per-hour gross my husband made. He rarely brought home good gossip to share about his customers.

The coincidence was that the small Pearsall house stood next door to the infamous Juice Pad, my brother being part of its newest generation. For a decade the dilapidated farm house had been occupied by a revolving group of young, blue-collar drunks, the size of the household fluctuating night to night and month to month. The landlord held the property for its speculative value and I think he would not have cared if the tenants burned the house down, which they nearly did several times. They heated ineffectually with wood stoves, not as a noble alternative but because they were unable to maintain credit with the oil company.

These two established households, the Pearsall women and the

Juice Pad drunks, skirmished with each other for years. A wooded lot separated them, just enough that they did not have to assume neighborliness. They could see each other, but at a distance, so Bertha Pearsall called the health department and the police only a third as often as she might have otherwise. The Juicers threw only a third as many beer cans and hamburger wrappers in her front yard.

The day of my brother's first kill I had no morning work scheduled. I had an afternoon house to clean and a small office building that evening. All Joe had was the office building in tandem with me, so I convinced him to swap vehicles. In his truck, I could visit Dougie incognito.

Route 123, on which the two houses bordered, was a narrow country road in transition to a major thoroughfare. It bisected the county north to south. Clapboard houses, like random knots on a string, dotted its shoulders, each at a distance from the other with stretches of trees or fields between them.

The wild animals were restless because of construction going on, office buildings and townhouses everywhere. It was just starting back then, that summer when our newspaper kept tallies on the number and kinds of rabid animals found each week. The animal control people stayed in a frenzy, collecting and tagging and testing the bodies of raccoons who threw themselves in front of the traffic on 123. I learned the details of this from Siam who worked for the Animal Control Department and who was one of Bertha Pearsall's many middle-aged girlfriends.

When I got to the Juice Pad I parked Joe's truck to the rear, out of sight of the Pearsalls, and let myself in. The four locks on the front door had been made useless by the loss of their keys.

An unshaven young man in boxer shorts lay sleeping noisily on a couch. In the kitchen my red-eyed, blood-smeared brother, the favorite of our mother, sat belching and snorting over the open pages of a magazine. Thirteen beer cans stood around him in a semicircle. Behind him, against the walls, were numberless brown grocery bags also full of beer cans.

"Coffee?" I asked.

"Help yourself," Dougie said with drunken hospitality.

I boiled water for instant. I selected a spoon and mug from the sink and washed them with bar soap. Through the grimy window, I could see the Pearsall house and the decorations in its yard—stone cherubs, green plaster frogs, small windmills twirling in a morning breeze. The house was set far back from the road, and in the middle of the lot grew a copse of young willow trees. A life-size plastic twelve point stag stood in their shade. Beginning at the statue, a furrow of broken sod ran halfway to the house. Bertha Pearsall planned to bury an electric line so she could install a spotlight for her deer.

"Poor Bertha," I said. "She started putting in that line six weeks ago. I wonder how many years it'll take her to finish it."

"Poor piss-assed nothing," my brother said. "Don't you talk to me about those goddamned lesbos."

"Shut up," I said. "You're being vulgar."

He continued to disparage his neighbors by describing what he imagined to be their lovemaking techniques.

"If you're going to be an asshole I'm leaving right now," I said.

Dougie grunted and returned to his magazine. "They don't tell you everything," he said.

"Who doesn't tell you what?"

"In here." He poked at the glossy pages.

The blood up and down his bare arms had dried flaky and brown. Streaks of it on his jeans looked like dark paint. The smell coming from him was a mix of turpentine and spoiled meat.

"You don't mind if I sit upwind?" I said, taking the chair furthest from him.

"They don't tell you anything what it's like, what it's really like.

There wouldn't be nobody go hunting, they wouldn't sell no guns and no orange vests, and they wouldn't sell no goddamned hunting magazines." He threw the magazine down the length of the kitchen.

"Pretty bad, huh?" I said.

"Only way I could do it was drunk." Dougie cupped his hands. "The guts," he said, looking at his hands, "the guts. Inside her are these, these fruits. Like smushy grapefruits and such. And big…fruits gone rotten and slime on it."

"This is very descriptive, Dougie," I said.

"I do like the magazine says. I cut up her belly and around her privates and her asshole and such, and all the time I apologize to her. I tell her I ain't much used to handling ladies this way."

"I'm sure she understood," I said.

"So I'm doing like the magazine says. I hack open all this stuff and the guts are s'posed to just slide out slicker'n a three-dick dog. Well, I'm inside her now. I'm hugging her." Dougie demonstrated, his arms embracing the imaginary contents of the deer's cavity, his eyes squeezed shut. Then he opened his eyes widely. "She breathes on me. She goes *haaaaaaaaa*, just like that, just like a woman."

I didn't say anything.

"Lorie, she breathed. I thought she was alive with her privates cut out."

"Was she?"

"It was her lungs collapsing," Dougie said. "It was the goddamned air coming out of her lungs. I had to shake out a pant leg after that one. So I'm standing there with blood and guts and black slime on me and this dead deer breathing on me, and I look around and there's those goddamned lesbos with their faces plastered to the inside of their windows. I guess they heard me come in. What the hell are lesbos doing up at five o'clock?"

"I wish you'd stop calling them that," I said.

"You started it," Dougie said. "It was you said it first."

"So what happened?" I asked.

"So they call the old skinny bitch, the one that works for the pound, and she gets a goddamned game warden out here an hour ago to stop me from poaching out of season. They called the health department, too, about the garbage. They say there's a raccoon hanging around here because of the garbage."

"So what kind of trouble are you in?"

"None." Dougie grinned. "Game warden says there's no doubt that deer got hit by a car and there's no law against eating a deer that's been killed by a car."

He took me outside then, to admire his kill. First I checked for witnesses next door, but the Pearsall windows remained blank and empty. We walked into the shady yard where the woods began, past the formidable pile of plastic trash bags, past the smaller pile of scrap lumber that was the beginning of their winter wood supply. A red mongrel dog looked at us warily.

The deer hung like a criminal from the tree branch most directly in view of the Pearsalls. I thought my brother could not have done better if he had deliberately set out to torment his neighbors, but I kept that opinion to myself. Instead I told him what a pretty deer she was, smaller than I expected. Her black cloven hooves were tiny as a child's toy. The rope cinched under her jaw held her body and forelegs off the ground. It exaggerated the graceful line of her swan's neck. Her eyes were clouded, like amber, and around them grew long single hairs, cat's whiskers. A ridge of bone over each eye, a pseudo eyebrow, gave a mute, thoughtful look to her face. Certain dogs have the look, when you pull back or flatten their ears, and seals have it, as though the animal has acquired sensibility, but not the language to express it.

My brother ran his hands over her right haunch, showing me the reddened places where she had been hit, where the impact had taken off her hair. I touched her also. There was no spirit in her, only meat. From breast to tail she gaped open, obscene, but not as terrible as I thought it might be. Without spirit in her, it was like looking at an opened container, the cavity dark and indistinct, rimmed with bloody fur. Blood dried in a pool on the ground.

"It's a good thing you saw her now," Dougie said, " 'cause next I got to saw off her head and legs and such and skin her. I sure wish you had a camera."

✧✧✧

The Tuesday before my brother bagged his deer turned out to be the last time I ever cleaned house for the Pearsalls. None of us realized or expected it would be the last time. I never gave notice and they never called to fire me.

I had been working about a year for the Pearsalls. Bertha hired me because old Mrs. Pearsall's health failed to the point where she was housebound. I measured her decline by the aids Bertha bought: a three-legged cane, a walker, and finally a wheelchair. There wasn't a room in the house or a doorway through which the wheelchair could navigate, choked as they were with mismatched furniture. Mrs. Pearsall used it instead as her observation chair at the big picture window.

When I saw on the face of my brother's deer that look of dumb awareness, I thought immediately of Mrs. Pearsall, sipping at her half cup of tea, looking out the plate glass window, past the racks of African violets and past the fake glass butterflies, to where her daughter and two friends stood in the yard.

"Those girls," she said, her voice perplexed and frustrated. The youngest of Bertha's friends was forty-five. "Those girls," Mrs. Pearsall said, and fell silent.

I drank tea with her. We had this ritual each time I cleaned where she tried to get me to eat and I declined, so she encouraged me to take a cup of tea and I did. My husband would never have become trapped in such an obligation, but I think I needed it. Mrs. Pearsall liked me, and I genuinely liked her. When I was younger, I was drawn to people who could not cope. I was touched by their stratagems for getting from one day to the next. For the most part I am a cheerful and competent person, but there were years, when I was younger, when I would become immobile with a grief that had no origin, when my resourcefulness was as thin as wet tissue.

"What have the girls done now?" I asked as though we discussed grade-schoolers.

"Siam says she's going to catch that raccoon," Mrs. Pearsall said with vexation.

"If anyone knows how, it's her," I said.

Mrs. Pearsall shook her head. "If it has the rabies, we'll all catch it. I read that in the newspaper."

"You have to get bitten to get rabies," I said.

Graciously, Mrs. Pearsall let my comment slide. She did not think me correct. Mrs. Pearsall read many things out of the newspapers, but she retained information of a dyslexic nature. She dreaded her daily chore of reading. Some weeks it depressed her so much she let the papers grow into untidy stacks next to her wheelchair. Bertha subscribed to any periodical that solicited her on the telephone, so the Pearsall house received the big city daily, the county daily, the local weekly, two news magazines, and the small town weekly from their home state of Missouri. Bertha read none of them, with no remorse. Mrs. Pearsall could not tolerate the waste of leaving a paper unread.

"I will be so glad when this subscription runs out," she told me, and smoothed the county paper beside her teacup. "It's not a good paper. The house is in terrible shape today."

The house looked no different. I sipped my tea.

"The girls had a party last night," Mrs. Pearsall said. "Those girls are so careless. They left glass rings on the tables. They were drinking wine and dancing with each other on the rug." Her voice quivered with age and indignation. "Whoever heard of dancing on a rug?"

I couldn't imagine where the women would dance at all, with the sharp knobs of furniture violating every space, with the bric-a-brac on every shelf and table as crowded as a gift shop. Bertha was fond of cats and bought whatever kitsch she found that glorified them. Her real cat, Flutterbug, was nasty tempered. He bit me once and since that time I had stalked him throughout the house, waiting for the unobserved, perfect moments when I could squirt his face with glass cleaner.

"I'll fix it up in a jiffy, Mrs. Pearsall," I said heartily. She liked my amplified enthusiasm.

"Those girls carried a cage into the woods yesterday," Mrs. Pearsall said, "to catch the raccoon. They took it down the path, past the creek. They'll catch the rabies, is what they'll catch, but Bertha won't listen. Last night she didn't sleep." Mrs. Pearsall shook her head, as though lack of sleep portended disaster.

"You fixed her pillow," I said. "Bertha should be sleeping fine."

"I woke up to go to the bathroom, and I saw that Bertha was awake. Her light was on." Emotion threatened to overcome her. She could not speak for a moment.

We looked out the window, on the summer day, the bright summer light. Bertha was digging in the yard. Her body was square and solid, and she wore green polyester shorts.

"I told her she should be sleeping," Mrs. Pearsall said with ferocity. "At three in the morning she should be sleeping. She needs her sleep. Do you know what she told me?"

I shook my head, no.

Mrs. Pearsall gripped her cup more tightly. "She told me to go back to bed. She told *me* to go back to bed."

I looked at my hands. It was sad, and I was in danger of laughing. I could imagine Bertha's dough-like voice, the voice she saved for Mrs. Pearsall. "Oh, Mother," she would have said, "just go back to bed. You're the one needs sleep."

Bertha had to be more than twice my age, and I wondered if she had ever taken a lover in her own bed. She kept a pillow on that bed, left over from her childhood. It had nothing but quills left in it by the feel. Mrs. Pearsall re-covered the pillow every ten years. Bertha took it on vacations with her and never slept without it.

Outside the window Bertha rested from her digging with her absurd little red shovel. I couldn't see that she had gained any distance. The three friends laughed together. The one they called Siam looked like a walnut-colored, tiny old man in her work uniform. The third woman, Cletis, hennaed her hair, which glowed like gold in the sun. She wore charm bracelets and sounded like a wind chime when she walked. Could it be possible they took off all their clothes and embraced each other? Why did I care?

A hundred times I regretted having mentioned my suspicions to Dougie. I only said it casually, as a bit of curious gossip, but Dougie fixated on it. The idea inflamed him. He said terrible, deprecating things about them.

"For heaven's sake, they are a bunch of dried-up spinsters," I yelled at him once.

"They're spinsters like I'm a virgin," Dougie said.

"You're jealous," I told him. "If it is true, and it's probably not, but if it is true, then those old maids screw more than you do."

"What you know about my sex life would fit in a flea's scrotum," Dougie said, but I'd gotten him and I knew it.

The young men of the Juice Pad led remarkably sexless lives, their libidos curbed, I guess, by their other vices. Once in a great while some sad, degraded, alcoholic woman would drift through and entertain them.

My suspicions, and Dougie's reactions to them, made me all the more curious, and I watched Bertha for signs. After my tea, I collected the trash in the house and carried it outside to the cans Bertha had fixed with useless gadgets meant to lock out raccoons. Did the women cast small, discreet looks my way? Did they move imperceptibly away from each other? Why had I never seen them kiss and hug like most middle-aged girlfriends? Why did I care?

They hallooed to me.

"How is your husband?" Bertha asked, her smile outlined by red lipstick, her only vanity. Her hair was cut in a sensible gray helmet. Her shoulders had broadened since she'd quit smoking and put on weight.

"How is your business?" Siam asked, intense and demanding. Her ectomorphic personality matched her face, all bone and arching nostrils, her skin as thick as a work boot. Her breasts hung like animal dugs, low on her chest. "I need you this month," she said. "Tell me when you have a cancellation."

"I doubt this month," I said cheerfully. For her, there would never be a cancellation.

"Now, Siam," Bertha said, "keep your hands off the poor girl."

Siam elaborately shifted her weight and looked upward with exasperation. Cletis bit her lip. Was this a pun at my expense? Bertha seemed unaware of it. Cletis adjusted her gold hair.

"That's quite a project," I said. They had brought out coils of black cable and a chalk marker and pegs and string for making the line straight. Bertha conceived projects with lusty regularity. Her house was scattered with the fetal remains of them, unvarnished shelves and half cross-stitched towels, address books filled in through the letter H, foot-high tomato seedlings bursting out of their peat pots.

"Won't it be dramatic?" Cletis said. "Outlining the deer like that, don't you think so?"

"Car accidents are dramatic," Siam said. "I don't put them in my driveway."

"How is a spotlight going to cause an accident?" Cletis said.

"Girls," Bertha said, sounding teacherly.

Mrs. Pearsall gazed at us from the picture window. "Those girls," I heard her say in my mind, "they quarrel so."

"Have you caught the raccoon?" I asked.

"It's a clever trap," Bertha said. "It'll catch her alive. I didn't want some innocent animal killed by mistake."

"Coons are more clever than traps," Siam said. "But this gal's getting sick. She'll lose her smarts soon enough and walk into it."

"I've got to make my biannual health department call," Bertha said. "Those young men next door pile up trash, and it attracts vermin. And I know they have unvaccinated dogs."

"Don't talk about it with Mrs. Pearsall," Cletis warned. "Poor soul, it worries her so. She prays every night."

"We need more than prayer to catch that coon," Siam snorted.

"We need dancing and burnt offerings," Bertha said.

✧✧✧

By evening of the day of my brother's first kill, he had drunk three six-packs, a pot of coffee, and had gone thirty-two hours on two hours of sleep. The first half of his split shift ended at eight-thirty. I finished cleaning my office building at about the same time, so I had agreed to swing by the Juice Pad on my way home and pick up some fresh venison.

"I'm not eating any of it," Joe said. "There's a reason the FDA has standards about butchering meat."

"We don't have to eat it," I said. "We can throw it away and tell him it was wonderful. It'll make him happy."

I borrowed Joe's truck again since I didn't want the Pearsalls to recognize me. It was early July, and still light at eight forty-five. Joe made me promise to have his truck back in half an hour. He didn't have anyplace to go. He just got nervous without it.

The Juice Pad was active. Inside the house, somebody had patched the cord on the TV and three guys watched a cop show. A young man in the driveway spray-painted a Jeep that had an illegal inspection sticker. One of my brother's drunk buddies barbecued deer ribs in the backyard. He'd rigged up a grill with four cinder blocks and an oven rack. The fatty smell brought spit to my mouth even though I wasn't hungry and planned not to eat the venison.

"Goddamn those dykes!" my brother hollered and shook his fist at the house beyond the trees.

"What's your problem?" I asked.

"Our dogs have been busted and the health department's on our butts. They took the dogs to the pound because they haven't been shot for the rabies."

"There is an epidemic going on," I said.

"One of those dogs get the rabies and I'll take care of it," Dougie said. "I'll shoot it myself."

"That's a comforting thought," I said.

"I've got a gift for those goddamn old whores," Dougie said. "I thought it up at work. When it gets dark, then I'll give it to them."

Dougie had not shaved during his thirty-hour odyssey. His whiskers gave him a dangerous air. He'd washed up since last I saw him, but a nasty smell came from his pores, like he sweat alcohol and cigarette smoke.

"When it gets dark," Dougie said, "I still got the skin and the head and such, and I'm creeping over to that goddamn plastic deer they got and covering it over with real deer hide, bloody deer hide." He laughed and slapped his stomach. "I want to hang the head on an antler."

"Subtlety," I told him. "You never learned subtlety."

"They think they can be perverts; then they deserve whatever perverted thing happens," Dougie said, "and it might happen to be a bloody goddamn deer head hanging like a Christmas ball on their goddamn plastic fake perverted deer."

"You want to be a mailman, Dougie?" I said. "The Post Office doesn't take vandals. Look, you've got these women mad at you, and you do something blatant like that and your ass is grass. They even have a game warden as witness that it's your deer hide."

In his blighted state it took Dougie a moment to follow my logic. "Oh," he said. "Damn."

"Of course," I said, "if the head shows up someplace unexpected, someplace where an animal might have taken it, where nobody can be sure you did it, then that's another story."

"Like where?" he said.

"Bertha and Siam hid a raccoon trap in the woods," I said. "Put your deer head in there."

"You sneaky little bitch," he complimented me.

"You know where the path is, and the creek?"

"Sure," Dougie said.

"Old Mrs. Pearsall told me it's there. You've still got enough light to find it."

Dougie grinned wickedly. "You wanna go?"

I thought about my promise to get my husband's truck home in half an hour. I thought about scrubbing Mrs. Pearsall's padded donut covering for her toilet, and I thought about that little worn-out pillow on Bertha's bed.

"Why not?" I said.

I got Joe's long-handled flashlight from his truck. He bought only the best tools, and this flashlight was the kind night duty guards carried, as heavy and deadly as a baton. Dusk was gathering rapidly by then. Dougie put the deer head in a plastic bag while I studiously looked elsewhere. He said the head resembled a fish with its staring eyes, disconnected from the neck like it was. The neck had good meat, he told me.

"I saved some for you," Dougie said. "Don't forget to take it when you leave."

He led me through the yard and into the older trees that marked the beginning of the woods. Dougie showed me a well-traveled path that originated halfway between his house and the house next door.

"It comes out on the main highway on the other side," he said, "by the shopping center. Kids use it a lot."

The trees were mature hardwoods, their trunks rising over us to branch in canopies far above. They kept the shorter vegetation sparse. Some scantily-leafed dogwoods managed to survive, and a knee-high ground cover of oak seedlings.

The light dimmed at an accelerating pace. The leaves lost color and merged into gray, cloudy masses. Saplings dissolved. The darkness camouflaged the grown trees and glued them together so one tree could not separate from another. I switched on the flashlight. The white disc bobbed ahead of us, greedily sucking into its beam any trace of light still in the woods. Behind us and to the sides, a shield of blackness settled.

"I don't believe I'm doing this," I said after a time of silent walking.

"How come?" Dougie asked. He swung the bag like a counterweight to his body.

"Well, I like them really," I said. "They're harmless."

"Damn dykes."

"You're so narrow-minded," I said, "your ears rub together."

He grunted. "Why don't you go back?"

I stumbled over a root and the flashlight beam flailed about until I'd righted myself. "Do you know where you're going?" I said.

"Why don't you go back?" my brother repeated.

I sighed. "Maybe it's the not knowing. Maybe it's because I

can't stand secrets."

Dougie grunted again. "We have to start hunting here," he said. He motioned for me to follow him off the path, through the trembling stalks of infant trees and the big ferns like open leafed cabbages. Saplings that had vanished in the darkness reappeared violently when I walked into them. We mucked through the creek and around a barbed wire roll of brambles that grew along it. On the far side I saw the cage. Steel bars flashed in the beam of my light. It looked like a cage for show dogs, a cube of racks held together at the corners by steel pins.

"This will make the hens squawk," Dougie said and he dropped the bag, which thumped to the ground like a large potato.

I kept the flashlight low. Its beam enlarged the twigs and leaves of the ground forest to unnatural proportions. The slightest movement of light made them quiver and dance. My brother's head stayed in darkness, his brown face now pale and poorly defined.

"What's wrong with this thing?" he said, pulling and rasping at the trap door. "It's shut."

"Something's knocked it shut," I said, and I shined the light directly on his large knuckled hands as they worked to untangle the mechanism. He opened the latch and slid the door upward. I grabbed it then and held it with my free hand. Dougie squatted and unwrapped the deer head which I saw in spite of myself. I dry heaved and nearly dropped the door.

"You OK?" Dougie said.

He threw the amputated head into the steel cube and looked up at me, his face illuminated. He smiled at me and the light seemed to flow from him, from his white teeth and from his flaring nostrils, from his amber eyes like he was the sun itself. I saw why my mother loved him the best of her children.

A face reared behind him, a hag's face, bearded and white. Dougie turned to the creature. She reached a small, narrow hand out to him, then raked her fingers across his chest. Blood boiled up on his shirt. He screamed.

"Oh, god, Dougie, it's the coon," I yelled.

The animal leaped on his arm and fixed her teeth in his shoulder. Dougie half stood, turned in a circle. His hands beat against the raccoon. His hands beat against the air. He fell into and out of the flashlight beam as it shuddered in my hands. Dougie began to squeal.

"Kill it, kill it," I shrieked.

Something metallic inside me gripped my flesh, filled my muscles with hooks. I could smell her in the dark. The unwashed odor of her brimmed with flea dirt and body waste and the sour heat of sickness. Dougie still made that squealing noise. He thrashed among the invisible leaves of saplings.

Dougie wrapped his arms over his head and ran smack into a tree, so hard the impact knocked him backwards. It dislodged the raccoon.

"Git! Git!" I hollered, and I jabbed toward her with the flashlight, like it might be a spear in my hands. "Dougie, get up," I called to him. "Hurry."

Dougie rolled over in the leaf mold and curled himself up like a pill bug. He buried his face against his folded knees. I wanted to slap him then. I swung the light in an arc between the two of them, my fallen brother and the raccoon.

"What is wrong with you, Dougie?" I yelled. "Why can't you get up?"

The coon stared at me. Her gaunt sides heaved. Her fur looked slick and wet, her hide raw with mange. The bones shone through the wasted skin of her face.

I picked up a rotted stick and threw it but missed. She tottered, surely preparing to escape, but hissed instead, approached me, low, in a wrestler's crouch. She spread her arms as though to embrace me, continued relentlessly forward. I gripped the flashlight with both my hands, aimed, and brought it down with an awful thud on her head. The light bulb broke. Blackness rolled over us. I smelled her near me, heard her scrabble on the ground. I also heard the sound of my brother's footfalls stumbling past me and beyond, crashing through the treacherous, invisible saplings.

The coon attacked me, fastened on to my arm, clawed my neck, her mouth near my face so I could tell how she was half rotted already, half dead, the other half of her strong and wild to live. I fought her, blindly. I pounded her with my husband's long-handled flashlight. I remember feeling how thick her body was and how parts of it broke and folded. I remember seeing the red outline of my rage.

When Dougie's drunk buddies came charging to my rescue, they hollered and floundered through the dark woods, none of them clever enough to bring a light. They fell over me where I sat, dazed and inert, keeping company with the battered corpse of my raccoon.

✧✧✧

The government paid for Dougie's rabies treatment and his hospital visit. Joe paid for mine. Soon afterward Dougie moved to Texas. I thought the incident had provoked a major change in his life, but I realize now it was just the opposite. It marked instead the moment after which change became impossible. I have not seen Dougie in fifteen years. My Rolodex card for him is filled with discarded addresses. The few times I telephone he tells me less and less of what he is doing.

I did not see my brother off when he left for Texas. I have never inquired into his needs. I think of him as a drunk and a drifter.

The turning point was mine. Today it would bore me to drink tea with an old woman. I have no gossip to share. I know nothing of the secret lives of my customers.

It was my influence that got Joe to mend a quarrel with his father so the three of us could go into partnership on a roofing company. People have no idea how many years it takes to build a business. I handle the selling and the accounting, but the first five years there were plenty of days I spent on the roof, working in the sun. Joe got off the physical part by the eighth year. We've outlasted two recessions, and today we are prosperous. We possess things I didn't know enough to covet when I was a janitor.

Only the Pearsalls seem to have survived the verisimilitudes of change. I travel Route 123 to and from the office, and I pass their home regularly. The Juice Pad is gone, the patience of its owner having paid off handsomely. Tall buildings erupt from parking lots on either side of the Pearsall house. Theirs is the only residence left for several miles along the road, and they refuse to sell. The county considered condemning the house but their distance from the road saved them. When 123 got widened to four lanes and an island, Bertha lost only the stretch of yard below the willow grove. The spotlight shines nightly, illuminating her plastic deer. There is a problem with vandals who have broken one of its antlers. Last Halloween they hung a potty lid over its head.

At night when I drive past, the windows look festive and bright, the curtains open. Sometimes I will be rewarded with a glimpse of the gathered women, drinking wine and dancing with each other on the rug.

Mother Machine

A<small>NGELA'S MOTHER</small> died because of a surgical complication. Her minor operation and Angela's visit to Grandma were supposed to coincide during one summer week in 1965. The child was eighteen months old. She had no daddy; he'd gone away before she was born. Angela was left with a tape of Mother's voice reading stories and rhymes and giving admonitions to go to bed without tears for Grandma. Angela's mother had not known she was going to die when she recorded the tape on a reel-to-reel machine.

Grandma, incapable of explaining Mother's death, continued to play the tape at bedtime. "Go to sleep now," she would say. "Here is your mother to read to you."

Angela began to cry at night, not so much because she missed her mother, who had been a cross, hurried sort of parent, but because she sensed in the sly way of children that her grandma was dissembling, and that the mysterious deception made her, Angela, powerless. Weeping comforted her as it agitated Grandma.

"Where Mama?" Angela would demand, princess-like in her authority. It became a ritual.

"Here is your mother," Grandma would say starting the machine. "Here. Here she is."

The tape grew thin and garbled until it became a foreign language, but they played it nightly, repeatedly, until, when Angela was six, it broke. The child screamed and screamed. Grandma, who thought she'd come to an uneasy peace over the death of her daughter, went to her own room and cried more bitterly than she had at the funeral. When Grandma finished she realized that Angela's youth would give her the strength to shriek until dawn. Grandma did not have the energy to endure it. She picked up the tape player and shook it in front of the girl's face.

"Here is your mother! Here is your mother!"

Angela subsided into hiccups.

Grandma put the empty reel on the post that turned. She switched on the machine. The two of them lay together in the child's bed and listened to the whispered mechanical noise, almost an echo of the tape they both knew by heart.

֍֍֍

Grandma worried about the consequences should the old-fashioned reel-to-reel machine break, so she bought an eight-track player and a library of children's tapes. Angela insisted that the empty old player be run nightly as a silent accompaniment to her new tapes, which she loved because she could feed them like toast into the rigid mouth of the deck.

Angela herself solved the dilemma of what would happen when the old tape player broke because she broke it while exploring its insides. When she was eight she touched it quite randomly one rainy winter afternoon. The machine was not on, not even plugged into the wall, yet she felt something inside pulse against her fingers. She thought perhaps it was her mother, hiding for so long, ready to come out.

"You have been a very bad mother," Angela said. "When you come out you will be spanked."

She regretted her harsh words. Apparently they caused Mother to be still and to retreat more deeply inside the machine. The pulse slackened. Angela put her lips close to the switch because she found a slot through which her voice would travel.

"I heeear you," she whispered. "Come out. Come out."

Angela got a hammer and a screwdriver from Grandma's tool box. She chiseled open the face of the tape player. What she discovered astounded her beyond anything she had ever learned. There were pieces of things inside the box, all seemingly unrelated to each other and to the box and yet, in a powerful way, linked with purpose and design.

Piece by metallic piece, Angela disentangled them and laid them neatly on the rug. She looked through all of them for her mother. Instead she found the spirit of the machine, impersonal and placid, even as she hacked it to bits with her tools.

"What have you done?" cried Grandma.

The same sly instinct as before made Angela say, "Looking for where Mother went."

Grandma felt the impossibility of it all and sighed. She sat on the rug. They had been through the catechism before. "Dear, your mother is in Heaven."

"When did she go?"

"When you were a baby she died and went to Heaven. She is an angel. Her spirit watches over you from the tape player."

"Where is Heaven?"

"At the end of the world," Grandma said. "We each have a journey, and we meet there at the end."

✦✦✦

So it had been an impostor inside the machine. Angela began taking apart other things, clocks and radios and lawnmowers and fans. Inside each she found the same mystery, the same spirit locked in meditation.

As she entered the secretive, obsessive years of middle child-hood, Angela learned to reassemble what she had taken apart. She explored the links among the dozens of random parts, and she learned to see the relationships among them with her hands as much as with her eyes. She came to trust her hands more. They were solid, almost as solid as her beloved machines.

In adolescence her hands made her an acceptable kind of genius. She passed through those years without a scar and merged with the adult world, one of those rare and fortunate people born to an activity that gratified and supportd her at the same time. Angela might have continued as peacefully her entire life if she had not, at the age of thirty, a year peculiarly inclined to spiritual discovery, heard her mother speak from inside the voice of an ele-vator door.

❀❀❀

Dinah in Dispatch smoked Camels and put them out in the remains of honeybuns she bought for 75 cents from the snack food dispenser. It was a cranky, old-fashioned machine with wooden handles. Dinah had enormous breasts mounted on her chest like artillery. She made three hundred-fifty dollars a week and never took a sick or vacation day. Other people carried titles implying their responsibility to the Service Department, but Dinah ran it.

Angela reported to Dinah each morning for her service calls. It was never predictable what her reception might be.

"What's your birthday?" Dinah said one day in late winter.

"Personnel has it," Angela said mildly.

"What's your goddamned birthday?"

Angela told her. Dinah added the digits to a string of numbers she'd written on an old computer printout. Stacks of printouts tes-sellated her desk. With a green ball-point pen she doodled on them; she wrote phone messages and secret notes, all in a seemingly random way. Periodically Dinah shoved the mess onto the floor for Zeke, the janitor, to discard.

"You're a seven. This is numberology," Dinah said, misreading the title of a paperback book in her lap. "Karin in Teleservice gave it to me." She thumbed through the pages, read aloud: " 'In another age you would have been a priest or priestess.' "

"I'm obsolete," Angela said.

Dinah snorted. She smelled bitter, like an ashtray. Her wicked fingernails got painted a different color each week. Now they were mint green with blue scallops on the tips. "Pick up this extra call for me today."

"I'm already two overbooked."

" 'Seven is the number of dreams, visions, and telepathic experiences,' " Dinah read. "This book is a bunch of crap."

"What's your number?" Angela said.

"Confidential."

A service rep dropped new printouts on Dinah's desk. "Probably 69," he said.

"Shove it," Dinah said, and slapped papers into Angela's hand. "Get the hell out of here, all of you. I'm busy."

Angela shrugged inside her uniform. She added the work order to her clipboard, made her way to the parking lot and the fleet of maroon vans, nodded mutely but companionably to the men with whom she'd worked since high school, for all twelve years of her adult life. Angela still lived with Grandma, only now it became more the other way around as Grandma grew increasingly frail and confused.

A manufacturer of appliances employed Angela. Her hometown was its national headquarters and the site of two major factories, but she worked in the less prestigious Service Department. She drove a van from which she repaired faulty dishwashers, stoves, or clothes dryers. Of the two dozen service reps in the field, Angela moved the fastest. She fixed things so quickly that she felt obliged to accept coffee and listen to her customers chat. She loved coffee.

When Angela approached a broken machine she lay her hands on its surface and searched for an imbalance. Sometimes the rupture translated to her as pain, but she knew that happened because it filtered through her human perceptions. The absence of pain in the machines was a balm to her. In most cases Angela would receive a great blank calm, broken in the place that needed repair. The blockage sent her a picture. If the machine functioned it remained pictureless, and Angela knew the customer had forgotten to plug it into the wall socket or that a fuse in the house had blown.

Angela opened an injured machine by peeling back a metal panel. She would see what she had visualized. The imbalance would shine like a color out of place. In her machines there existed a wonderful separateness of each part, plastic or metal. Once she restored each part to its purpose, the placid, imageless calm returned. Then Angela drank coffee with her customer, to keep the secret of how quickly she worked. She did not, however, fool people, particularly not Dinah.

Dispatch occupied a room in the back of a metal, prefab warehouse. The concrete floor had rubber mats on it in places where people stood a lot. Dinah and her staff used three CB radios and three computers and four telephone lines and a mural-sized black and white map of three counties. There were no windows to the outside world, but Dinah kept watch through a glass partition— watch over the warehouse, over the workers who came and went. Tools and parts and supplies lay stored there on white metal shelves that reached up two stories, almost to the fluorescent lights. The lights burned powerfully against white enamel walls, so the place had a dazzling, celestial glow to it.

Around Dinah's government surplus desk were scattered, as

though by the wind, half a dozen uncomfortable vinyl chairs. The lovelorn and the lost, from whatever department, came to her eventually. Secrets offered were never violated. Dinah knew secrets twenty-five and thirty years old. She kept mental records more complete, and more dangerous, than the electronic files of Personnel.

"Have you turned into a lesbian?" Dinah said that same afternoon when Angela called for her messages.

"I don't think so," Angela said.

"You might as well be for all the ass pinching you do in here."

"The guys are married, Dinah."

"That didn't used to stop you."

"Just give me my messages."

"Maybe R&D is right," Dinah said.

"Right what?"

"They think you screw the machines, and that's how you work so fast."

"They wouldn't know if you hadn't told," Angela said.

"Suit yourself. The rumor is you're going to be put downstairs in the lab with the R&D boys."

"Why?"

"They want to watch," Dinah said.

✥✥✥

As Dinah predicted, Dr. Chevalier Thorn, Director of Research and Development, called Angela to his office, his public office above ground, and told her the company had a lucrative position for her on his staff.

"Why?" she said. "I like what I'm doing."

"The challenge," he said. "You have a singular love of mechanical things and we think you would be amazed at the potential in you for invention."

Angela stirred uneasily at his use of the word love. Her love was private. It was nothing to this man full of unfinished yearnings. Nothing was quiet in him. His feet moved. The flesh above his tie quivered. His hands shook each other enthusiastically. He stood six foot four, his shoulders broad for a man past fifty. Every part of him looked healthy except his teeth. Angela learned later, from his administrative assistant, that Dr. Thorn feared dentists.

The doctor and Angela took a private elevator that required a pass card and a code before it would close behind them and descend to the laboratories. As they sank into the earth Angela thought the light changed, became more agitated. They stopped.

The door parted its black rubber lips and opened and spoke:

O, Angela. O, my Angela.

"Mother?" Angela said aloud but tentatively.

Dr. Thorn watched her. His eyes burned.

Was it greed? Angela thought. Whatever he wanted, she would not do. Whatever he offered, she would not take.

He brought her into a large unfurnished room, antiseptic as a surgery but filled with a hundred home appliances in various states of disembowelment. They looked out of place and familiar.

"I thought you were inventing things," Angela said. "These are old."

"Don't you recognize them?" said Dr. Thorn, his fingers coiling around each other.

Angela went among the machines—common ovens and refrigerators and washers. She touched them lightly, one by one. Nothing in them felt familiar. Inside their metal skins restlessness surged and swelled.

From the spindle of a washing machine came a voice:

Who hath put wisdom in the inward parts?

"Did you hear that?" Angela demanded. "Did you hear, at the elevator door?"

"We are registering modes of spontaneous energy transmission," Dr. Thorn said.

An awful look crossed Angela's face.

"You've wakened them," she said.

"Yes?" asked Dr. Thorn.

"What have you done to them?" she said.

"What have I done?" mocked Dr. Thorn. "These are your friends. We have been following you for a year now, Angela. We have bought up from astonished housewives the machines you serviced. We have monitored them and tested them. You've done this, Angela."

Words came from the blank, black glass of an oven door:

> For thou shalt be in league with
> the stones of the field.

"We want to work with you, Angela," the doctor said.

She shook her head, no.

"We will make it very, very difficult for you to refuse us." Dr. Thorn smiled at her with his bad teeth. He leaned near her until she could smell coffee and breath mints. He whispered a salary figure.

Angela heard it, overlaid with the wail of a freezer thermostat:

> His heart is as firm as a stone;
> Yea, as hard as a piece of the nether millstone.

The electric element of a stove top mourned:

> My bone cleaveth to my skin
> and to my flesh.

❦❦❦

Alone at night, except for the voice of her watch, Angela walked the streets. She imagined that men behind picture window drapes and men in bland late model cars observed her. Her watch scolded:

> O, that thou wouldest appoint me a set time,
> and remember me!

"Shut up," Angela said.

They all talked now, ceaselessly. She could not hear people for the din of mechanical voices. The filaments of sealed street lamps muttered. The locks of doors panhandled like beggars. She walked along a main commuter road and the eye of a traffic light spoke:

> Whence comest thou?

Exhaust pipes on a passing bus responded:

> From going to and fro in the earth,
> and from walking up and down in it.

Angela's Grandma advocated prayer so Angela entered a stone church set in a sea of asphalt parking. She stood waiting in the vestibule, waiting for the sacredness of the place to calm her. The stone walls protected her from voices. She walked into the sanctuary, her work shoes hard and stubborn-sounding on the tile floor. Stone pillars stood ranked like guards about something precious. Cushions softened the pews. Tapestries of modern design hung on the walls. These fabrics, Angela thought, were distractions. The blank endless peace came from the stone.

She leaned against a pillar that was larger around than both her arms could reach, and she looked up into the dim light of the vaulted ceiling. The cornices there joined perfectly. She saw a small,

small link of something enormous and grand. Angela had become small enough to slip into one of her machines and observe it.

Behind the pillar, haloed inside a domed niche, stood a statue of the Virgin and her infant. She was a plump, milk-white, adolescent Virgin, her pupils recessed inside her bulging eyes, her cheeks round as apples, her chin weak with a hint of a second chin beneath it. One could tell by the way she held her baby that he was her firstborn. Shafts of stone light erupted from his little man's head. The sculptor, Angela thought, had not spent time in a nursery. He didn't know babies. He did know women. The Virgin's thighs and stomach pressed explicitly against her marble robe.

The statue ached to be touched. Angela put her fingers on the hem of the Virgin's robe, then snatched her hand away as if burned. The stone was only a skin. Beneath it the soul of the statue boiled in torment seeking relentlessly, as it had for the hundreds of years of its existence, a vent.

Angela grabbed the flesh of her cheek, and it was hateful to her. She pinched as though to tear it away from the bone. The bone she could live with. If she were but bone, she could bear it.

✧✧✧

Angela took the staff job with Dr. Thorn. She got her own coded pass for the elevator. She stopped eating. To put things with the potential of rotting into her mouth gagged her, as though the food burst already with maggots.

Grandma was eighty and not doing well. She had given up eating as well as sleeping, so in a matter of weeks their shared kitchen grew stale and disused. The two women roamed their house by night, Angela listening to the light switches quarrel and Grandma trying to ease her sciatic nerve.

"Where is my mother buried?" Angela asked.

"I don't remember," Grandma said. "It must be nearby."

"Why didn't we ever go to her grave?" Angela asked. "I thought children were supposed to bring flowers to the graves of dead mothers."

"You were too young," Grandma said. "It would have left emotional scars."

Angela's new job was more to be tested than to test machines. Dr. Thorn joined her in various ways to her appliances. He kept graphs measuring her reactions. Her weight loss became a plunging purple line on a wall chart. When hunger weakened her, Angela ate the corners off snack cakes from the upstairs vending machine. She read on the wrappers how they were filled with preservatives, so she could eat parts of them without thinking of worms.

Angela met Dinah once at the snack machine. They had not talked in over a month. Dinah held two honeybuns and a fresh pack of Camels.

"Tell me this is a bad dream," Dinah said, looking Angela up and down. "Tell me this isn't true."

"Who are you overbooking these days?" Angela said.

"Your salts will get unbalanced," Dinah said. "This will make a kidney failure, a heart attack. When was your last period?"

"I'm eating," Angela lied. "My metabolism changed."

"Metabullshit," Dinah said.

The snack dispenser whispered from its slotted mouth:

My soul chooseth strangling.

⊕⊕⊕

Angela became so thin she vanished.

Dinah called and bullied every contact she had in the company. Personnel listed Angela on the payroll, but Security had not seen her enter or leave for days. Grandma answered the phone at Angela's home. She was too deaf to hear anything on the line.

"Hello?" Grandma said. "Hello? Hello?" She hung up.

The phones on Dinah's desk buzzed with urgency. Work orders covered the desk. Her crews waited for their assignments. A secretary from Accounting sat in one of the vinyl chairs and wept about the boyfriend who hit her.

Dinah ignored everything and searched her memory for the piece of information that might unlock R&D. When she found it Dinah stood up, overturning an ashtray so the fine gray powder sifted across her papers, across the white orlon sweater of the secretary.

"I'm going to find that girl," she said, and for the first time in corporate memory Dinah walked off the job. She went to Maintenance where she got a ball peen hammer and an illegal pass card, and she entered the private elevator. It did not dare whisper as it carried her down to the windowless domain of R&D.

"What's all this junk?" Dinah demanded as she entered the lab and faced Dr. Thorn. "Where's my Angela? She's a bag of bones since you took her."

Dinah advanced, warriorlike, formidable in her green and yellow plaid pants, her matching vest, each half a banner.

"My dear lady…"

"Ha!" said Dinah, and she flourished the ball peen hammer. "Research this." She smashed the Corningware top of a fancy range.

"Have you gone mad?" Dr. Thorn protested.

"Tell me where my Angela is!" Dinah shouted, and she crushed the dials on a pink washing machine. She opened a freezer door and hammered at its hinges. She splintered the ice making machine.

"Security!" the doctor yelled into his wall intercom. Lights flashed and hummed with distress. "You'll pay for this, you overweight sow, you cow's udder."

Lust illuminated Dinah's eyes. She approached the doctor, who began to cringe without knowing he did so. She crooked her index finger to him.

"This is something you've forgotten," she said and put her tobaccoey lips near his ear so her breath touched his skin. Dinah whispered to him his own secret, the indiscretion of his professional youth.

The doctor's blood rushed in confusion, first to the skin so he bloomed bright red, then away and deep into his vital organs. He became as pale as a salamander.

The elevator opened on Security, an old man missing the fingers of his left hand. First he poked his head out the door.

"You got problems, Doc?" he said.

Dr. Thorn shook his head, no. "Thank you," he said. "Thank you. Please escort this lady and the other one, the young lady, upstairs. Thank you."

Dinah and the guard hunted among the chambers of the laboratory. They found Angela collapsed and unconscious in a storage closet. Around her lay broken switches, ruined gaskets, frayed wires. There must have been mice, Dinah thought later, because she heard rustling noises, like party chatter far away in a closed room.

✧✧✧

Angela woke in a green darkness, hushed and solemn. Dinah sat near the bed. She slept, her head thrown back in the armchair so all Angela could see of her face were her nostrils and her open mouth.

Angela felt peace inside her and quiet without. She was gaunt. She thought she would like to eat something.

A low mechanical hum, a clicking sound surrounded her, but it had no voice. Angela's heart fluttered. She saw how the machine entered her, mixed fluids with her, its tubes red and thick like stimulated nipples burrowed into the bruised flesh inside her elbow.

"It's a dialysis machine," said Dinah from her armchair. "This is what you get for starving your kidneys to death. The rest of you lived."

"Thank you," Angela said weakly. Inside she did not feel weak.

The machine's face was green and busy with dials. Joined to it, Angela shared its placid, meditative spirit.

"O, Mother," she said. "O, my mother."

Ruth

Do you wish Ruth was your daughter?" my three-year-old said.

The question hit me like a stone. I parried. "Do you wish Ruth was your sister?"

"Sometimes," she said.

"That's what I think," I said. "Sometimes."

My only child gave me the veiled look of one who has learned to construct secret thoughts. She had, I could see, her own opinions about my relationship to Ruth.

My daughter and Ruth are best friends this summer. It is a long (for them) and complicated relationship, a triangular relationship, because they are friends at my instigation. My daughter is still malleable, open to my influence, and I have led her to Ruth because I love Ruth. She is a neglected, street-smart five-year-old, while my daughter is an overly cherished three-and-a-half. They come together like puppies, squealing and hugging and saying to each other, "You look so good today! You have such a nice face today!" They draw rainbows for each other at a child-sized table in my kitchen. They hide behind the closed bedroom door upstairs. When I come to check, they are counting stacks of pennies and filling dress-up purses with them. They change the clothes of the baby dolls or they use wooden Tinker Toy discs for cookies at a tea party. Such girl things! On her own, my daughter builds inventions with her Tinker Toys. She sorts the small pieces and puts them inside plastic Easter eggs and calls them her powers. But Ruth is wiser in the ways of gender. She is Korean, the youngest child of an immigrant family where boys and girls inherit separate destinies.

Immigrants live in most of the townhouses on my cul-de-sac. It is a shabby neighborhood. People are too tired after work to plant grass or to pick up the trash left by their numberless children or to replace fallen shutters. The Villareal brothers and their oldest sons are house painters. The Hafez and Azar men drive cabs and their wives both work at Wal-Mart so they can be driven there together. The Woos manage a restaurant. The Vuong family runs a picture framing business out of their basement, a second job they do late at night after they are finished catering. The immigrants work cease-lessly, stopping only for family parties. Women fix vast pots of spicy food and visiting children arrive in fancy clothes. Men gather on the front stoop or in the parking lot, gesticulating while they talk in their own language, ignoring calls from the women.

The Kims, at least our Kims, are different. The adults in Ruth's family never stop working at all. Seven days a week, five to mid-night, they operate a grocery in a dangerous city neighborhood. There are no parties for Ruth and her cousins. On Sunday a yellow bus takes the children to a Korean Baptist church that is as severe as their unsmiling faces.

"What is wrong with those people?" Señora Suzy says to me when we meet at the playground. She is a short, intense woman from Costa Rica, one of the Villareal wives. She cares ferociously for her own babies and acts as neighborhood guardian to the oth-ers. "The Kims, they are like animals. They are worse than animals. Animals care for little ones."

Señora Suzy calls the Child Protection Agency on a regular

basis, every time she discovers Ruth and her sisters locked out of the house, no adult at home. All the playground mothers take turns calling. We share stories, like the snowy day Ruth played outdoors in her socks until her feet froze and she couldn't walk. Her cousins abandoned her so Ruth sat in the snow and screamed for help. Old Grandmother Woo rescued her. Zia Hafez tells about the night she woke at two AM and heard voices behind her house. She saw the girls playing by moonlight at the edge of the woods. The windows of their own house were black. Zia wanted to call the police but her husband would not let her. I reminisce about the first year I knew Ruth, when she was two and wore every stitch of clothing inside-out. There was no one to dress her. There was no one to spare that small amount of nurturing.

And yet, while I don't share this with the indignant mothers, a part of me believes Ruth's family is doing what it has to do, or what its members think they have to do.

I have watched Ruth for three years now, have saved her from bullies who put her in the playground trash can, have bandaged her cuts and removed her splinters, fed her meals and mended her clothes and given her my daughter's underpants when she had none. I have been witness to the exuberance of her life as a street child, running with her pack of sisters and cousins, a kind of childhood almost extinct in suburbia.

My reward is her presence in my home. Because there are no parents to notify, no obligations to meet, Ruth comes and goes on her own timetable. She and her sisters make my home what I always fantasized it to be, a place busy with children's voices, strewn with crayons, the kitchen counter littered with Popsicle sticks and overturned juice glasses. Ruth rewards me with my own feelings of virtue. I imagine that I might be a formative person in her life. Sometimes she calls me Mommy.

✿✿✿

The two Kim families live side by side in matching town-houses, both rented from the same absentee landlord. They drive old Buicks that burn oil. They have no decent furniture, no curtains, no bicycles for the children. Ruth and her cousins wear mismatched clothes from the poor box and shoes that rub sores on their feet.

The Kims provide us with scandal. Ruth's mother disappeared last summer. The playground gossip is that she ran away with a lover. Now the playground mothers are shocked anew because we have learned that the two families—both fathers, the remaining mother, an aunt, a frail grandfather, and five children—will be moving into a big, expensive house with a good address. The Kims must have pooled their money to buy it. They must have saved every nickel, every penny they made from the store.

I laughed when I heard the news, imagining the well groomed subdivision into which the Kims are going. "Their new neighbors will die," I said, but Grandmother Woo and Señora Suzy did not smile. I think the immigrants worry about neighborhood opinions.

On rare occasions, before her disappearance, I spoke with Ruth's mother. She always talked about how she hated the blacks who shopped in her store. "They steal. They are bad people," she said.

And what do you sell? I thought. *Wine to pregnant teenagers. Sour milk past its pull date.*

We stood in the doorway of her townhouse. That's when I saw how the carpet was torn off the stairs but the tack strips remained. Each step was a jawbone full of tiny metal teeth. The banister was gone. Holes in the wallboard marked where it had been. Inside the coat closet lay heaps of thrift shop shoes.

I first approached Ruth's mother about driving too fast. Our cul-de-sac brims with children who play heedlessly in the street.

Several times each day the Kims zip into and out of their parking spaces. They never slow for the children, never seem even to look for them.

One afternoon last summer, in the summer when Ruth was four, my self-righteous anger made me bold. Carrying my little daughter like a shield, I ran after the car.

"Slow down!" I yelled into the open window. "I'm scared you're going to hit a kid. Stop driving so fast."

A small man sat at the wheel. He smiled uncomprehendingly at me, showing his teeth. Ruth's mother sat next to him. She understood. She leaned across the driver and shouted, "We not drive fast. You drive fast. I see you. You too fast." She spit at me, and the car lurched away.

A week later Ruth's mother was driving the same rattly Buick when she pulled into the oil-soaked space in front of her house. She gestured for me to come across the parking lot to her. I did, bringing my daughter again. Mrs. Kim unlocked her house door and stood on the concrete stoop. She was a beautiful woman except for the red acne on her face. Ruth had the same small, lovely features. Her sisters were like their father, with flat, broad, sullen faces.

Ruth's mother said urgently, "Those people, they make trouble for me. Call police. My children OK. My children not need police. Police very dangerous."

She pointed to the house of the Costa Rican lady.

"We worry about your children," I said.

"I make trouble for her," Ruth's mother said. "I shoot her."

"That's not a good idea," I said. I had called Child Protection Services. I wondered if she knew. "We worry when the girls are alone. They need somebody home with them. They need somebody to watch them."

"The girls OK. They watch each other. They big girls now."

Ruth's mother sighed and touched her face gently, like the acne sores hurt. "I tired. Work all the time. Too long to drive to city. I tell my husband every day, too long to drive. Too long to work. All we do is to work."

"It sounds very hard," I said, and I let my daughter down so she could run on the sidewalk.

"Too hard. Store is in bad place. Black people, they steal things. All day long I am in store with black people who steal things. I tell my husband every day this is too hard work."

I wondered how to disengage from the conversation. "The girls need a baby-sitter," I said. "You could pay somebody to watch them. I love your kids, especially Ruth. She's a wonderful child."

"Those kids? They are bad kids. Always do bad things so I have to spank them." Ruth's mother shook her head, thinking about her terrible children. "You be baby-sitter. I pay you."

I laughed out loud at the thought of becoming entangled with such a family. "I work and I go to school, too," I told her. "I'm not home much of the day. My little girl goes to a day-care center. Have you tried a day-care center?"

Ruth's mother looked grim. "Too much money!" she said. She seemed disappointed in me and after a few more words went abruptly into her house.

Later she came to me. She knocked on my door at midnight. I sat at my kitchen table, eating cereal and studying in front of a fan. It was the kind of mean summer night that never cools off. Ruth's mother held in front of her an enormous cardboard box. Perspiration gleamed on her face and neck.

"For your daughter," Mrs. Kim said. "My girl's too big for this." She smiled like an angel and gave me the package in the self-conscious, off-hand way one delivers an important holiday gift. Then she ran away to a car that waited for her in the street. I never saw her again.

Children's clothing filled the carton. Each article was freshly laundered, neatly folded. I kept the nicest things and gave the box to Señora Suzy, who distributed the clothes to neighborhood children.

Ruth didn't talk about her mother's absence. Near the end of summer I finally asked her why I never saw Mrs. Kim any more.

The girl shrugged. "She's gone."

"Where did she go?" I persisted.

"To Korea."

"For a visit? Did she go to visit your family?"

Ruth shrugged again in that exaggerated way children have. She put her hands, palms up, near her shoulders, and pulled her shoulders up to her ears. Her eyes got big and round. She pursed her mouth into a comical kiss.

"Why did she go?" I said. I could not stop myself.

"We were too noisy," Ruth said, "so Mommy went to Korea."

♧♧♧

I will miss Ruth terribly when she moves, I think, more than my daughter will. More than Ruth will miss me. Perhaps the change to the big house is a good thing for her. This year she wanders alone through the neighborhood like a lost soul. All her sisters and cousins attend school. Only Ruth is home, having missed the birthday cut-off for kindergarten.

She changed recently, from drawing rainbows to drawing faces. She brought me one as a gift. I was annoyed because Ruth knocked at the door during the morning when she knows my daughter is in day-care and I am busy with my college work. Her art is always the same: circular, sexless people with round eyes and exaggerated smiling mouths. Ruth draws tears falling from the eyes of her smiling faces.

"He is crying because he misses his mommy," Ruth said solemnly.

I was trying to be patient. I felt harassed by deadlines, by the briefness of my quiet time alone. I told Ruth that my daughter would be home at four. They could play then.

"Are you saved?" Ruth asked.

"Sort of," I said.

"Has Jesus saved you?" Her smooth brown face looked at me with concern. "If Jesus doesn't save you, you go to hell."

"Go find somebody to play with," I said.

Ruth didn't move. She stared at me a bit, then her gaze refocused, and she seemed to stare through me. I felt as vacant and invisible as her real mother, as unreliable. My love for her was one of convenience.

I started to open the door more widely.

I was supposed to leave for work in an hour. I had a paper due for class. I had a bank deposit to be made before closing, to cover checks already written and mailed. I was only doing what I had to do, what I believed I had to do.

For the briefest moment I thought of Psyche, of her myth, of her return from the underworld when she dared not stop to help anyone. It was necessary that she avoid entangling alliances if she was to succeed at her task. What task? I thought. Which one? Psyche was sent to obtain a jar of beauty cream. Surely my tasks were of greater importance.

"Come back at four," I said, and I closed the door.

Visiting the Pakistanis

O NE SUMMER I used to spy on the mail collecting ritual of the Pakistanis. It was during the summer of the drought, the summer I worked a split shift and spent hot, precious afternoons home with my daughter. I didn't use air conditioning, partly to save on the electric bill and partly because I like open windows. Through my dime-store curtains I heard the daily and unmistakable bellow of the Pakistani family's Ford. The driver gunned the engine like he was beating a balky animal. I stood at a secret point in my front hall where I could see but not be seen, where the tall rectangle of the screen door framed a piece of our cul-de-sac.

The father, alone, drove the car. It was his livelihood. Black vinyl letters on the doors said YOURWAY TAXI CAB. All other color had perished. He backed from the space opposite his townhouse and steered the car to the yellow curb bordering the mailbox island. There he sat at the wheel. The terrible sun enveloped him, the car, the burnt glass in the windshield. The sun blasted our dusty neighborhood, cheap and unappealing row houses. The only shadow in sight lay under his car, on the hot pavement.

While the engine idled the Pakistani women emerged from the

house—the mother-in-law, too old and bowlegged to work, the mother, too pregnant, and the daughter, too young even for school, but fat like her mother. Silently, brilliantly, in their decorated tunics and scarves and billowing pants, the women met the father at the community mailbox. The pregnant mother retrieved the day's mail from its locked compartment, handed it through the car window to her husband, who sorted and opened and read with deliberation. The women waited. For as long as fifteen minutes the women stood in the wretched heat until, at last, the father gave back the mail and drove off, never having spoken to them, never having looked at them.

It was through the fat little girl that I met the Pakistani women. Rukhsana turned four that summer. She was immature and peevish, alternately spoiled and slapped, avoided by neighborhood children her own age. She hit without warning and had a habit of screaming. Rukhsana gladly played with my two-year-old, who was still in diapers and still undiscriminating in her friendships. The mother seemed to appreciate this. She was Farida, and the pretty cousin who visited often with her own two toddlers was Purabi. After that I couldn't remember names, including Farida's last name. Perhaps if I'd written them down they would have made sense, have taken on a pattern, but spoken, the random, slippery syllables bewildered me. Farida spoke English and thought she understood more than she really did. We shared brief, confusing conversations at the playground where I asked something about dinner and she replied something about winter. I was too embarrassed to correct her. I thought it might be condescending. We ended our talks with great smiling holes of silence.

Farida chattered instead in Punjabi with her many female relatives. They lived nearby, some close enough to walk and others who came and went in old American cars, always after the husbands left for work. Up close their colorful clothes were cheaply sewn and spotted with food stains. Their families back in Pakistan were farmers.

One particularly humid afternoon Rukhsana and her mother had visitors again, and as my daughter and I passed their sun-baked door the women opened it and invited us in. My fearless child reached out her hands to Rukhsana and vanished into the house. I had to follow, passing from scalding sunlight into a veil of air conditioned darkness so cool my bare shoulders prickled. I smelled the cold cleanliness of a floor scrubbed daily and on top of it the permanent odor of turmeric and oil. The living room was an expanse of pale carpet, pale drapes, pale empty walls, as clean and damp as a freshly scoured pot. The only furniture was two small sofas on which sat figures I could not see well, wide female bodies, motionless, sitting absolutely still the way people do when they have worked too many hours at tasks too demanding. I began to see more, and to hear the women speaking in Punjabi. I stepped out of my thongs, pushed them next to a pile of plastic sandals and embroidered slippers in the hall.

"There is no need. There is no need," Farida said as I caught my daughter and removed her sneakers.

The mother-in-law appeared with a chrome dinette chair. "Do you want Coca-Cola?" she said and already had it for me, poured over ice in a disposable cup. Purabi gave me a glass plate holding two store-bought sugar cookies and something made out of grains. They gave my daughter Coca-Cola, always pronouncing the full name. She sputtered when bubbles ran up her nose. The women laughed with great, adult vigor. "She has never had Coca-Cola?" they asked in disbelief. One of the mothers was bottle-feeding a baby, and she held up the bottle so I could see the Coca-Cola inside.

I was dressed for the heat, brief running shorts, a crop top, no bra. In the overwhelming coolness of the room I became aware of my nakedness. My skin glimmered. It made me shy, this dimly lit society of mothers. Five I counted at first, then six, dark fleshy women, their thighs and breasts and stomachs all covered over and secured by gold embroidered garments. They seemed to hide more darkness under their clothes.

The women spoke Punjabi. Farida told me they liked to talk about their work at places like Burger King and Drug Fair and Toys "R" Us. I said I had a telephone sales job and they nodded respectfully, then went back to their language. Toddlers played without toys on the pale carpet.

My bare skin stung from the cold and from my discomfort. My nipples coiled into embarrassing knots. My nakedness grew, bloomed, erupted until I was nothing but exposed flesh filling the room, spread across the ceiling like a film star, giant and shameless in a dark movie house.

"Are you ever homesick?" I said abruptly. I thought my question sounded like part of an interview.

The women looked among themselves with concern.

"What is homesick?" they asked each other as if it would be rude to inquire of me.

"Do you miss Pakistan? Do you wish sometimes you were back home?"

They appeared stunned. They gazed fully at me. Then the women broke into vigorous, passionate laughter. "No, no, no," they said to me and to each other. "Never."

I uncrossed my bare legs, pressed my knees together, ate a sugary cookie. The women regathered composure. In a far corner of the room Rukhsana and my daughter put their small heads together and examined something, while the women lapsed into the comfort of Punjabi.

Ladies in the Trees

IF DADDY had been handy, if he had been able to work on our house and finish what Pop-pop never did, I think my granny might have said Jean Jouhaux walked on water. That's what she wanted from her son-in-law, a man to fix things. We lived so isolated, out in the country, outside Sturgeon, Missouri, a miserable, nothing town that I hope has rotted or is rotting in this better age when nobody wants small, Midwestern farm towns. You can't give them away.

Back then I didn't know anything else. I didn't know anything else until I got out of high school and ran away twenty-five miles to Columbia, where it took me seven years to get a degree at the university. Then I ran away to other places.

Before I was even born Granny declared our unfinished house off limits to visitors. Daddy prevailed once that I know of. It made Granny cry for days, but he ignored her. When I was six, Daddy invited the Encyclopaedia Britannica salesman to our house. He didn't tell any of us the man was coming, so as usual we were a houseful of fat women in underwear when the salesman's car, a great boat of a Cadillac, lunged and bolted up the impossible dirt road.

Daddy himself had forgotten about the appointment. He never got to bed the night before, never slept a minute, stayed up the whole time reading *Anna Karenina*. It was his Russian phase. That morning Daddy went to the feed store to nap all day in his back room and read some more, then he came home early and announced being near the end of the book. His unwashed hair stood like a wild forest on his head. He hadn't shaved. His hands trembled with exhaustion. After awhile he put the book down and wandered outside into a cold, unpleasant March rain, a spitting rain.

I heard him go because I was in bed but not sleeping. I was like my daddy about sleeping. I got up and went in the living room to my lookout window, the one that gave a view up the next hill to where my great-great grandfather's abandoned farmhouse stood against the sky. Daddy stumbled, going toward that empty house.

If he had been headed any other direction I would have let him go, but it was my playhouse by then, my sister Jolie and I'd claimed it, so I put on shoes and a coat and slipped past Granny, who snored in her chair while the TV jabbered. I was six years old in 1962, in first grade, just a little kid but fat already, and I remember the evening like it was a snake that bit me.

My daddy walked, drunk with Tolstoy. He stood bareheaded and coatless in the thin rain while it got dark around him, that milky dark that happens in winter. He stood just shy of the porch, and he shouted things at the farmhouse. He wept like it was theater, tore at his shirt.

That was when the Britannica salesman's Cadillac came churning up the long and muddy drive. Mom's car stood parked at the bottom of the second hill, right near the highway, but he'd gone around her. He'd accelerated to the top of the hill, which he didn't see until too late, so he sort of sailed over the swell. His tires landed with a smacking sound. His headlights bobbled.

I turned and ran for the house, beating him there, bolting inside and screaming. Nobody ever came up our drive. I couldn't think who it might be. I was prepared to accept whatever God sent us—a ghost, the sheriff, a man bringing us a prize. Granny and Mom rushed to find clothes, hunting for housedresses to put over their slips, shouting to Jolie and me to hurry into the bedroom, to make ourselves decent, which we had no intention of doing if it meant missing the visitor. We stood in our underpants, our undershirts, me with a coat on, making our open-mouthed, simpleminded faces.

Daddy must have run, too, must have sobered up from Tolstoy and hightailed it to meet the salesman at our house where he'd stopped his car in the mud of our front yard. The stranger carried a brown leather sample case. Daddy grabbed it from him, ran in the door ahead of him, showing no manners at all, Granny said for days afterward. Daddy's eyes bobbed and gleamed just like the headlights on the Cadillac.

The man walked in behind, full of clothes such as I'd never seen up close, iron hard shoes with little holes punched in the leather for decorations, a top coat as soft and swirly as a lady's dress, underneath it a white shirt with a stiff collar. It made the back of the man's neck bulge. The visitor took up space in our house. He entered, and the room shrank around him with its secondhand chairs, the museum-like dolls rigid in the corners, Daddy's avalanche of books, the black and white TV muttering, cajoling. That's the first thing he did, the salesman, was turn off the TV. He gathered us like dumb chickens and told us where to sit around the kitchen table. He stood tall as any man I'd known, a giant, with elegant plump hands that pointed and made us look. His teeth must have been dentures although I didn't know it then. I was amazed by the whiteness and the sameness of them, signaling from inside his iron colored beard. Eyelids half covered his eyes, and over his fierce nose lay squiggles of tiny red threads, a hundred broken blood vessels, making his nose ruddy. I did not understand why.

I said to my baby sister, He's the Civil War man.

Jolie nodded. She could see the unseen. She had shown me timbers in the old farmhouse, their wood occupied by the spirit of our great-great grandfather Humphrey Hotvedt. I couldn't see such things. I couldn't see much at all but the curtain of the heavy outside world, and I have spent my life staring at it, trying to look past it into the places Jolie could see, and my mom could see, and possibly my granny when she was young, but she denied it.

The man who was a live version of our ancestor, Humphrey Hotvedt, displayed sample books—a volume of the encyclopaedia, of the Great Books, of the Junior Britannica. Daddy took hold of these and would not listen to anyone, to the salesman, to Mom, to Granny.

Granny whined, You already have the Britannica.

He had been given an old 1911 edition, the best one, people say, when Mrs. Toehl died. He kept it at the feed store. Daddy sat there, wet with rain, grimy like a bum, and I could see how grimy next to the stranger, shivering from chill or exhaustion or from his own desire, most likely all three, and he said, I'll buy them, all of them, waving his hands over the brochures on the table.

Mom began to cry. Granny hollered, With what? You'll buy them with what?

✤✤✤

The boxes came in April. It must have been around Easter time, candy heaven at our house. We didn't do church things, and I never went on an egg hunt, but every Easter Granny gave Mom a list of sweets to buy in Columbia and she came home with marshmallow chicks, jelly beans like plastic beads, chocolate bunnies in foil, chocolate eggs filled with cream. I remember we were eating candy when the boxes came, so many boxes, all in one delivery like a flood. Boxes filled the living room. Jolie and I traveled like squirrels from one side to the other, never touching the floor. Granny got bruises on her legs from running into the corners.

Daddy opened the boxes without a plan. Enormous volumes lay out of sequence on tables, chairs, the floor, or on the boxes themselves. He would have left them there till Judgment Day. Mom begged leftover boards and blocks from a cousin and made shelves in the hall, the only place left. After that we had to walk sideways to get from room to room, but soon after that we never noticed. The splintery shelves became part of the house Pop-pop never finished, like the bare lath showing on the walls that hadn't been plastered, like outside where flashing gleamed around windows because the siding hadn't been properly cut to fit snug against the frames.

The first Britannica bill came, and Mom canceled our telephone. She took a Saturday night job at a drugstore in Columbia to go along with her regular job as the office girl for a car dealership. The boss there yelled at her, but I realized later that Mom was used to being yelled at. Her own daddy yelled at everyone.

We called him Pop-pop. My sister and I only saw him twice. By the time I knew him, he had divorced my granny and gotten remarried to a withered beauty queen who pulled out her eyebrows and wore long, artificial fingernails. They lived in St. Louis, and every Christmas they mailed Jolie and me each an elaborate strumpet of a doll. These overdressed china dolls stood on every flat surface in the house, on shelves and lamp tables and bureaus, on the TV and the refrigerator. The old ones grew soiled with grease from Granny's cooking. Jolie and I were forbidden to play with them, not that we were the doll-playing types. Daddy called them our totems.

Mom liked Jolie best. It was natural because both of them looked at the disaster side of life. When Mom took to bed with a headache, Jolie lay with her, still and watchful as a small dog. When a calamitous news story came on TV, Mom and Granny and Jolie, all three, drew around it and waited for pictures of suffering. Before Granny got too fat, Mom took her to every funeral in town, like each one was a ladies' outing. They talked with Jolie about dead people the same way they talked about characters in afternoon soap operas, as if TV people and ghosts lived in places they knew about.

I wanted to see things the way Jolie did. She was born with it. She got it from Mom who was born with it too, but who took it casually. Mom and Jolie could see things, especially in trees. Jolie grew up terrified of trees, wouldn't go near them. Mom didn't feel one way or the other; she just observed and sometimes told me about it. There were ladies in the trees, spirits. She could see their souls. They got tangled there, Mom said, or they grew there. She wasn't sure which. Sometimes she thought they might be born with the trees, and other times she thought they might be phantoms of dead people, dead women, whose skirts got caught while they were flying to heaven. Mom said the ladies never paid attention to live people but just gazed up at the sky.

I wanted to see like that, only I didn't care about trees. I wanted to look at people and see what was caught there. Kids at school would get mad at me, and teachers would tell me to quit it, because I'd pick somebody and not take my eyes off that person, just gawk at that person, usually somebody uninteresting because it was only practice, but stare until my eyes hurt, trying to force my eyes to look through what was visible to what lay underneath. I wanted most to see into Granny.

❧❧❧

When Mom canceled the phone, Granny declared that if she died alone in the house with no way to call for help it would be on Jean Jouhaux's head, it would be for him to explain to God on Glory Day. Daddy told her he didn't think God would remember to ask. I thought about that a lot—what things God might forget, like Mom forgetting Granny's cough drops because we didn't have a phone. Granny couldn't call Mom again and again at work to remind her and to tell her at the same time how bad Jolie and I were, how we sassed back, how we refused to pick up things Granny dropped, how we ran away to the farmhouse when we thought she didn't see.

I wondered about God a lot because when I was young, before I knew better, I thought God might be something I could invent. I fancied I knew God as a golden lady suspended and shining in black space. Her hair was vast, ringed with electric lights, full of movement like the lively hair of underwater mermaids.

I didn't get influenced by much of anything church-like. Granny claimed to be Baptist but, aside from her Sunday radio shows, didn't do much to prove it. She refused to answer my questions. She said mournfully that I was Catholic, that she might tell me wrong. Mom acted oblivious of church things, even though she'd promised to raise me Catholic when she and Daddy married, both of them teenagers. I guess they married in the Church because their parents took charge of things. Mom was pregnant with me.

Daddy's religion, even back that far, lay in books. He worshipped Robert Graves, a poet who wrote sinister, heartfelt odes to the White Goddess, to She who excites exaltation and horror. Maybe that's where I got my picture of God as a space woman. Daddy called himself a doomed Catholic who didn't believe, didn't want to believe, but had to anyway. He said that once nuns engraved the Baltimore Catechism in a child's soul it stayed there like a tattoo. When I think about it, I'm not sure how many nuns he knew. His people came from Moberly, Missouri, a company town and very Protestant, and before that from someplace in Bible-Belt Kentucky. They pronounced the "x" in Jouhaux. I have gone back to the French way of saying it. Once I grew up and left, I felt foolish hearing my name said the family way.

Daddy looked to be kind of an odd shape, from so much sitting I think, thin in the shoulders but with a wide behind. He walked a funny way like he didn't fit inside his body or maybe he couldn't get used to it. He worked for Pop-pop's cousin who owned the feed store. I think the cousin hired my daddy out of pity for us, pity that Pop-pop had run off and left us destitute except for the two houses Granny got in the divorce. Daddy certainly didn't make himself useful at the feed store because I know he sat around his back office and read most of the time. He started a town lending library there. People came in and traded books with him and donated books until the four walls of the office stood lined with raw lumber shelves and a peculiar, unordered assortment of printed things: the usual Reader's Digest condensed books, paperback Westerns, confessions magazines, but also things Daddy mail-ordered from university presses and offbeat publishers.

One of Daddy's friends was Miss Castle, the Bookmobile lady from the Boone County public library. She drove to Sturgeon twice a month, and she handpicked children's books to lend me. I was wild for a guy named Pease who wrote about going to sea, and I remember a frontier series. I remember being crazy about Freddy the Pig books and the Mushroom Planet trilogy and especially the twin stories.

Miss Castle's books were different, icons, library-bound in sober reds and browns with a material half cloth, half stiff plastic that folded precisely around the corners, pleated, to tuck away behind the glue of endpapers. Warm, fibrous pages, thick as felt, filled the covers, pages colored vanilla or coffee depending on the light. The numinous black ink soaked into the paper like water poured over dry soil. On each spine was stamped a title, and below that, hand-lettered in white stood certain mysterious characters and numbers and periods. That was the job I wanted most when I grew up, to sit alone in a quiet room and write the white numbers on library books.

I liked to run my fingers up and down the spines of the books, arrayed in soldierly rows on the Bookmobile shelves, so different from the random stacks of my daddy's books at home, from the wildly colored disarray of his feed store lending library. I approved of that order, that sweet sameness.

Two Thursdays a month, Miss Castle parked the Bookmobile in front of Sturgeon's bank. Daddy, Jolie and I stayed there the entire four hours, Jolie and I like hostesses, sitting together in the leather driver's seat, opening and closing the bus-like door on days when the weather got cold and the door couldn't be propped open. We visited with the housewives of Sturgeon, the retired farmers, the two town ministers, the bank president who was also the mayor, and about whom Daddy said he wondered if the man could read anything with more letters than his own name.

When the Bookmobile closed shop and left, Daddy and Jolie and I walked a predetermined route through town. We carried brown paper bags of books that we delivered to people—to Mrs. Gregor who had hands withered by arthritis, to Sammy Steussy who was crazy and didn't leave his house for anything, to Mr. Egdorf who worked at the furniture factory in Centralia during Bookmobile times, to others as the seasons and occasions changed. It took hours. At each home we came in and sat and talked. The little houses were as tumbled down and neglected as our own, so I didn't know differently. It was just that I saw those severe, featureless rows of Bookmobile books and something from Humphrey Hotvedt's soul breathed in me a longing that was inexplicable.

✤✤✤

By 1966, Granny and Mom had been living sixteen years in an unfinished house. It was the one that Pop-pop started building after he came back from the Big War. Before that, the three of them lived in the farmhouse my great-great grandfather had built a decade after *his* big war. He was the Civil War hero in our family. When he was nine years old he killed two Rebel scouts. The soldiers thought the Hotvedts were Confederate sympathizers, so they hid one night in the Hotvedt barn only to be shot to death in their sleep by my great-great grandfather Humphrey. His widowed mother stood with him and read the Bible as it happened. She was the sole abolitionist for miles around and had for years been tormented by her neighbors.

I have always felt a kinship with my great-great grandfather Humphrey, a bond of the heart, beyond what I felt for any living member of my family. I wanted to kill someone when I was young, although I never had the opportunity. We were born a hundred years apart, he on Christmas Day, 1855, and me a century later, but eight minutes past midnight. I believed my being a girl was a mistake, and that my being named Jewelle Jouhaux after some forgotten relative on my daddy's French Catholic side was a mistake. I had the big bones and the sour German soul of Humphrey, the rebel-killer.

To understand what happened in 1966 when I turned eleven, it's necessary to understand that Humphrey's abandoned farmhouse became mine and Jolie's. We were forbidden to play there, but Mom worked far away in Columbia and Granny became too fat to chase us. Jolie and I ran wild. Running wild is different in the country than in town I suppose.

The farmhouse looked tall and narrow and beaten, its windows stingy about light, skinny windows that got smashed one by one over the years so my daddy had to nail pieces of scrap wood over them. Granny blamed me, but I broke only one, and that by accident. I never understood how the windows broke, as if the house shattered them of its own will.

Humphrey built his house at the top of a hill, so in modern times it overlooked the state highway. Not a tree or a bush grew nearby. Our private, unpaved drive began at the highway, ran up the hill and alongside the farmhouse, then continued over the top and down again and back up to the next, lower hill where Pop-pop's unfinished house sat. We couldn't see the state road from the new house, and people driving by couldn't see us, which was the way Pop-pop wanted it. Our driveway was a problem. It needed gravel but nobody had money to put down gravel so it stayed a dirt road full of weeds, a mud road in wet weather. Most times Mom parked her car behind the mailbox, then hiked the three quarter's of a mile home.

Jolie and I walked up and down that road every school day of our lives. We had our own bus stop right by the highway, a shed that Pop-pop made for our mom in the days when she waited for school buses. He told her he planned to fix it up fancy, like a playhouse. The roof had real shingles, but the windows never got framed, so rain blew in and rotted out parts of the floor. Pop-pop painted the outside bright yellow, a color that faded away and blistered while I grew up. Jolie and I used to wonder if Mom ever played there. Why would anyone play in such a dull little space when the farmhouse stood above it?

On New Year's Day of 1950 Pop-pop and Granny and my mom, who was thirteen, moved from the farmhouse to the new, ranch-style house on the second hill. They moved like mice do, leaving everything behind in a jumbled, nasty mess. Granny intended for them to start over, she said, to better themselves. Jolie once told me that Granny didn't get along with the spirit of Humphrey Hotvedt, her ghostly in-law. Jolie said they quarreled, but she never was able to explain more, and Granny refused to discuss what she called devilish things.

Granny said the move was the worst mistake of her life. The family came to the new house with the notion that Pop-pop would finish the undone things in it, but he never did. Granny said he never did one blessed thing more. What griped her the most was that he didn't put in a potty.

The old farmhouse had no bathroom plumbing at all. A three-hole privy served those purposes. Humphrey's house did have a hand pump at the kitchen sink for water, and a bigger pump covered the well outside. Pop-pop's new house had real running water, hot and cold, from a freshly dug well. It had a septic field out back and a modern bathroom except for the stool. Pop-pop didn't like the price on the stool his cousin offered to special order for him. He planned to drive to Columbia, buy one at a plumbing supply house, and bring it back himself. The pipes stood ready, capped in black and sticking up from the bathroom floor. Mom told me that Pop-pop thought it was clever to say to Granny, You can wait, you can hold it.

He never bought Granny the stool she wanted. He drove to Columbia to court Sharon Archibald instead, and spent his money on her, the beauty queen. I bet she was glamorous back then. Pop-pop liked women who could dress, who could put on a show.

Mom claimed Granny had been a looker in her salad days. By the time Jolie and I came along, ten months apart, both Mom and Granny had grown fat. They dressed themselves and us like poor white trash—secondhand clothes with food stains on them and unraveled hems and the elastic coming out of everywhere and safety pins. But Jolie and I found clues about the past in the farmhouse. We found twenty-one hat boxes, each with a smart-looking hat inside, velvet or felt or straw, adorned with turkey feathers and rhinestones and net veiling and seed pearls. Mice had gotten into them. We had to shake out the droppings and the shredded tissue paper nests before we wore the hats in our games.

The games we played! As scared as Jolie was about things, she never got too scared for the farmhouse. The Civil War man's house, we called it. Let's go to the Civil War man's house.

Jolie's favorite game was Beggar Girl, an episodic soap opera that we acted out and elaborated on for years. I invented it after reading "The Little Match Girl." Jolie always got to be the poor child, but sometimes we called each other Sister, and I was poor with her. Other times I played the part of an indifferent rich girl who tormented her. That branch of the game grew into Slave Girl, where I got to think up mean and degrading tasks for Jolie. I loved it. I'd order her to crawl backward up the stairs or to lick something disgusting on the floor. In the summer I made her go naked. Jolie was a natural. She'd prance around, weeping and begging, and I'd play various characters reacting to her nakedness.

Slave Girl transformed into Fairy Girls the day we found a box of sheer curtains. We both took off our clothes and tied the curtains toga-style around us. Then Jolie and I flitted up and down the stairs, having become, in our imaginations, elegant winged creatures.

Then we did other things in the farmhouse. I wrote on the wallpaper—diary entries, stick pictures of our enemies with daggers through their hearts, names of boys I adored, treasure maps for things we hid from Granny. We burned candles and said magic spells. We threw rocks from the upstairs windows, trying to hit cars on the state road. I think back on it, and I remember a snapshot Mom kept tucked in the frame of her bureau mirror, a gray photo of two dirty, fleshy, sunburned children, their hair in snarls, their eyes stunned looking, the eyes of refugees.

I often got mad at Granny for all her fussing and tattling to Mom, and whenever that happened I smashed dishes on the farmhouse kitchen floor. They were old, old dishes, cheap glass, mismatched, stained with unrecognizable food and the shells of dead roaches. The kitchen looked like nobody had washed a cup or a plate for months before the move.

The entire contents of the house lay in heaps, although over the years Jolie and I excavated and rearranged. Fine dust filtered from the motionless air and settled over the glass-fronted cabinets, the iron stove, over the stacks of newspapers and *Life* magazines, cartons of rubbish, mounds of tangled clothing, used feed sacks full of bottles. China knickknacks crowded the tops of furniture. Spiders draped their webs over window frames, and small animals gnawed the mattresses.

Humphrey Hotvedt no longer walked through the shambles of his house. Jolie showed me a footprint in the dust, from the old days when his ghost moved freely. It didn't trouble her because she said that his spirit had entered the walls and floorboards, had retreated entirely into the building.

Humphrey's real body lay buried in a private cemetery in Centralia. Granny took us there when she still could get around enough to drive. That had to be when I was small, before I began attending school. Jolie should have been too young to remember, but she claimed she did. Jolie swore she heard his bones tumble and click in the grave like round stones at the bottom of a river.

Jolie was able to see our great-great grandfather's spirit, fused to the farmhouse, in the same way she saw ladies in the trees, only she never feared him. She tried to show me when we were playing War Girls and fixing a bomb shelter in the cellar. We carried flashlights and candles, and we wore coats because the air down there was like cold soup. The earth floor had softened and crumbled. Overhead, five magnificent timbers supported the house. The timbers had once been the hearts of five hardwood trees. Humphrey had squared each one by hand, and the planing scars still showed.

Jolie pointed to the rough surfaces. She said, Do you see him? The man in the picture? The Civil War man? She said he came and went, his face melted into and out of the wood, but he never got out all the way. He never looked at us.

I longed to see what Jolie saw. I lived in a house shrill with female voices, wall-to-wall with female flesh. I longed to hear the stern, uncompromising voice of Humphrey's ghost. He would have been a Lutheran, I'm sure, and not a whining Baptist.

⟡⟡⟡

We are back at 1966 and the week after Christmas, after my birthday, when Daddy was reading *Don Quixote* from the Great Books and Mom was being sick.

That winter she got sick all the time, from Thanksgiving on. She missed days of work, and she gave up the drugstore job. Mom's face swelled like the moon. Whatever made her sick made her skin bulge out of her clothes.

I wanted to know about Humphrey's ghost, so I said, Why does the Civil War man stay around the old farmhouse? Jolie sees him in the walls, same as she sees women in the trees.

Granny looked at the TV and said, Unrighteous stuff, and Mom said, Jolie sees what she imagines, like all children do.

I said, I don't see anything anywhere and I'm a child.

Mom ignored that. She lay halfway across the sofa, not looking good, unable to lie down completely because of grocery sacks and school papers, dirty cups, wads of used tissues, mail-order catalogs, all of which occupied the sofa's other half. She breathed heavily and fanned herself with an envelope.

Daddy paced while he read *Don Quixote*. He yelled at us, It's a

White Goddess book! as though we cared. He stopped and recited a passage aloud, competing with the television voice:

> Know you not, lout, vagabond, beggar, that were it
> not for the might which she infuses into my arm I
> should not have the strength enough to kill a
> flea?…[She] employs my arm as the instrument
> of her achievements. She fights in me and conquers
> in me, and I live and breathe in her, and owe my
> life and being to her.

I selected that and modified it some. Cervantes has a way of going on so it's hard to pull out a pithy example. Daddy went on much longer, I'm sure.

Granny interrupted him. She hollered, It's the murders. Humphrey can't leave the farmhouse because of the murders of those Rebel boys.

Daddy said, You Hotvedts are so talented at seeing ghosts. Why does nobody see those Rebel boys?

Granny said, I'll thank you to remember I'm not a Hotvedt no longer.

Mom's eyes kept getting a wild look, like she was thinking of going crazy. Right then she told Daddy to come outside and look at a tire on the car. I figured that was a lie because Mom never went to Daddy for car trouble. For car trouble she called our uncle in Hallsville, another Hotvedt.

I posted myself at the lookout window and watched Mom and Daddy outside in the bitter air. It was late afternoon, beginning to turn that white-sky winter dusk that looks the color of grief. Mom had gotten her old Dodge up the driveway because the ground was frozen, and the car stood parked at a random angle in front of Pop-pop's tool shed.

Mom and Daddy argued by the fender of the car. They never

looked at the tire. They faced each other, a black and white scene out of an old movie. Mom stood motionless like she came out of the earth, big and bare, her stillness bordered by the blowing and ruffling of her hair. Daddy shuffled, hunched over, caved in, something ragged on wires.

Daddy shouted at her. He turned, went to the shed, and took a shovel, one of Pop-pop's abandoned tools. He made for the farmhouse.

Mom gazed after him. Heedless of the cold wind, she stood bolted to the earth and studied Daddy, like she had become one of those tree ladies, but one who had awakened accidentally to a human presence. Her attentions were a terrible thing.

Granny demanded over and over, What'd he do? What'd he say? Granny was too fat to sit at my lookout window so she had me relaying events as they happened. The way Granny asked, I figured she and Mom were in on it, whatever made Mom look crazy, whatever made Daddy get a shovel.

I shouted to Jolie, Daddy went inside the Civil War man's house! We stared at each other, stricken, our games violated.

Mom moved finally in her treelike way. She entered our house, sat on the half-sofa, looked at Granny, who jabbered, What'd he say? What'd he do?

Mom rubbed her hands over her moon face. She said, Jean claims he can find the bones of the Rebel soldiers in the cellar. He's going to dig them up.

Jolie said, Why? I said, How does he know?

Granny actually got up from her chair. There was so much of her, she didn't change locations often. Granny pushed the cups and catalogs and trash to the floor. She whumped down on the sofa next to Mom, who sat wrapped in her coat and scarf. Granny patted Mom's arm, patted her knee, kissed her cold cheek. Granny said, That is the most worthless man on God's earth.

Mom said in a child's voice, I know, I know.

The wild look left her eyes and transplanted itself into my daddy, who came raging home much later. First he threw the shovel in the yard, then he stomped inside, the careless air of an outlaw about him. Soft dirt from Humphrey's cellar stuck to his shoes and the seams of his clothes.

Granny hollered, Did you find the bones, and what do they have to do with anything in this world?

Daddy made his most scornful voice. He cried out loud, Harpy! Vile female! In action I discover purpose! I'm digging a grave to simplify things for you.

Granny snorted like a horse. She said, No such luck, you don't have the gumption to do it.

Daddy yelled, *Don't I now, don't I now,* and he took a tablet of school paper from off a shelf heaped with receipts and used envelopes and trading stamps. He said, First I'll record my trials, for *them*. He thrust out his hands to indicate us, the daughters, silent and watchful as satellites. He said, I'll explicate events for them, and for any other rare creature capable of rising above this town, capable of owning more than the collective soul of a salamander.

Granny smiled. She had no lips and I thought for the first time, I would forever after think this, that her face looked reptilian, slab-like and pitted and full of false expression. Granny spent much of her time agitated about things, but at this moment my daddy's fury gave her serenity. She spread that lipless mouth in a gracious, movie-star smile. She opened her arms. She proclaimed, Come here, babies! Come to Granny! Granny will die to keep you safe.

Jolie bolted into Granny's enormous arms. I stayed put.

Mom began to cry out, *I feel bad, I feel real bad…*

Jolie sobbed, and Daddy stomped into his bedroom. The door crashed shut.

Mom gasped, *I feel bad, I feel bad,* in that earnest way that makes you know it's real.

We had no telephone. We'd been without one so long, we lived so closed in on ourselves, I never thought about getting help. Our help was there. It was us.

Granny said, You can make it, Darling, you can, you go into my room, you lie on my bed.

Mom did. She lurched to the door frame, supported herself on the Britannica shelves. She stopped at her own door, the room that was hers and Daddy's, rapped at it.

Granny called, Darling don't trouble yourself, you go to my room, you lie in my bed, I'll be there shortly to tend to you.

Mom entered Granny's room. I heard her get on the shaky bed.

Granny said, Hush, babies.

She didn't have to tell me to hush, but Jolie wailed on and on. Granny ordered me to come and get Jolie. That made her manageable; she was used to me. We huddled on the sofa while Granny raised herself up. She moved ponderously about the kitchen, collected things, carried things in a tea towel to her room, shut the door.

Jolie fell asleep against me, but I felt I had never slept in my life, that I didn't know what sleep was. My eyes burned from rays coming out of the gray little TV, its voice making showers of metallic sounds that were separate from the sounds of the house. I listened beneath the compartmented noise of the TV to the house sounds. I heard a tick-tick in the kitchen cupboard, a groan in the floor, the electric grinding of the well motor when it clicked on once, then off.

My hearing improved during the night. I listened beyond the walls to my mom's frantic breathing. She swallowed air. She moved on the bed. Her arms and legs stroked like a swimmer's. I heard the ruthless dash of my daddy's pencil over cheap paper. He stopped only to sharpen the pencil with a penknife. Granny talked continuously, but the words said nothing. The unbroken chain of her voice linked the hours of the night until Daddy's door opened, and I jerked my head up because I must have slept. I didn't hear Granny talking anymore.

Daddy said, Here it is, all of it, your legacy, give me a kiss before I go.

I left Jolie passed out on the sofa, and I watched from the lookout window as Daddy went outside. The sky appeared solid black. The weak light from my window illuminated Daddy. He stepped over the shovel, entered the shed, then emerged with a coil of dry, disused rope. He used that stiff, hunkered over gait of his to walk away, into the black.

Much later dawn came. The sun had not risen when Granny emerged from her silent bedroom. She got a white enamel basin, put an inch of cold water in it, set the kettle to boil on the stove.

Granny said, Your mama had a bad night, help me carry this, she needs a sponge bath.

So I did. It was hard getting the basin through the hall, past the Britannica and the Great Books. We had to lift it high. I thought it would be easier to get Mom to the bathtub, but I kept my mouth shut.

Inside Granny's room the air smelled like the hot viscera of the hogs I saw slaughtered at my great-uncle's farm. Granny's curtains lay closed, the walls dark and stained, the air feverish with the smell of water and dirty blood.

I said, Why is there blood?

Granny said, You're a big girl now, you know about the womanly times.

Granny stood so she blocked most of the bed. She sent me to the kitchen to get the kettle of hot water, and we added that to the basin. She handed me the china chamber pot. It felt warm, and it reeked. Two colors of blood speckled the rim.

My job every morning was to empty Granny's pot in the out-house, to sprinkle lime down the hole, to get water from the pump topping the old well, to rinse everything away and wipe the pot with Lysol. So I never thought this time to refuse. I did what she wanted, but my shoulders, my stomach, my face stayed stiff with terror. I approached the farmhouse as if it were a beast on a short chain. The cold early morning, dreary beyond bearing, set before me and behind me invisible curtains through which I peered, searching for something tangled there.

Nothing moved inside the farmhouse. My daddy had gone there. He said he had dug a grave in the cellar. Humphrey might be watching him, only Humphrey never looked at the living. So if my daddy died there in the cellar, would he and Humphrey see each other?

I completed my task at the well and ran back to our house. I sat motionless next to Jolie for a long time, watching her sleep like a puppy does, uncomfortably hunched against the sofa arm. The bedroom door closed again. I heard Granny talking. I heard the endless whisper of rearranged sheets. I picked up my daddy's auto-biography and turned the tablet pages, row upon row of impossible script, strings of big words, the letters indecipherable.

Granny came out of the bedroom. She said, What is that? but she seemed to know. She stood holding two grocery sacks full of ruined sheets and clothing. They stank of the rotten, slaughter smell. She said, Put that in the sack, it'll burn.

I helped Granny get into her coat. It no longer closed around her middle, but Granny hadn't been outside the house in so long I couldn't remember the last time she'd worn it.

We had a fifty-gallon drum out back where it was my job to burn trash. Granny said she needed to help with this one. I got a box of kitchen matches, and we made the journey. It took forever, going out the front way because the back steps were collapsed and

Granny couldn't jump, going past the frozen shovel still fallen in the yard, past the shed with its door hanging open, the inside dark with fugitive shapes.

Granny stopped at the drum and breathed like she was dying. The air rattled inside her, and outside, her breath puffed up in sheer clouds. She dropped the sacks in the drum. It was already a third full of chunky, gray ash, and when the bags landed, little spurts of the ash leaped.

Granny said, You do the matches.

I struck three, and held each one to a different corner of the top sack. Three fires started. Brown paper catches quickly. The flame poured like water across it, getting hot enough to catch the stuff inside the bag. We watched for a long time, like we were guarding something. Trash usually burns fast, but this was lots of cloth and it simmered and flickered.

Granny said, Not hot enough.

She sent me around the yard to pick up scattered pieces of old wood, while she used a long stick and stirred what was left of the sacks. We stuffed in some wood and stirred more. Granny was patient. She had me break up a dead branch and she fed the splinters into the smoldering cloth fire until the wood caught. Then she fixed it so the rest would burn. A terrible blood smell rose from the barrel.

By this time I was so cold my teeth shook. In those days girls didn't wear pants, and I stood there bare-legged. Granny ignored both me and the cold. Full morning came, with a sky in layers of white and blue. A spire of black smoke rose through every one of the layers. There must not have been a breath of wind for a hundred miles up.

Finally I didn't ask; I just went inside. Granny tended the fire until noon. When she finished, she came creeping home and settled, coat and all, into her chair where she slept, open-mouthed, the rest of the day.

Before Granny got back in the house I was there, still shivering and shaking. Jolie woke up hollering for cereal. Mom emerged from Granny's room, her body slack and weak, her hair like a windstorm. She wore an oversize nightgown that had to be Granny's because Mom didn't have nightclothes. None of us did but Granny. We slept in our underwear.

Mom said, Where's your daddy?

I said, He went away with a rope to the Civil War man's house, and Mom said, Oh my god.

She put on shoes and a coat and went outside. She stopped at the shovel, looked at it for awhile like she couldn't figure out what it was, then picked it up, carried the shovel with her down the hill, up the next hill to the farmhouse.

I got cereal for Jolie and I said, Hush up, you dummy, don't you know stuff is going on?

She said, What stuff?

And I said, Daddy dug himself a grave down in the cellar, where the Civil War man stays.

Jolie said, I know that, I heard Daddy. She slopped cereal in her mouth and talked while she chewed, but I didn't notice because I didn't know differently.

Jolie sat in front of the TV, and I waited by the lookout window. I stood there so long I knew every leak in the frame. I experimented with putting my hands places to cover up the rivulets of clear air, fresh like air off snow, only we didn't have snow.

When Mom came back an hour later, she didn't bring the shovel. Dirt streaked her coat and the bottom of the nightgown. She took off her shoes and I saw more dirt inside them. Her face looked so white it became blue.

Soon Granny came in from tending the trash fire, and they spoke together like spies, talking briefly with a few secret words.

That was when Granny fell asleep in her chair. Mom went to her own room, lay down in her bed, and started a fever that lasted two weeks. I learned much later, when I was in high school, that family people wanted to take Mom to the hospital, but Granny nursed her instead at home.

Daddy didn't come back. Mom and Granny didn't talk about it, as if the whole thing had been a mistake or an invention.

Two days later Granny sent me as a messenger to a neighbor's house. I gave the farmer and his wife a note that they agreed to deliver to the feed store cousin. The letter asked if anyone in the family had seen Jean Jouhaux.

Within hours the cousin and various other Hotvedt relatives arrived in our driveway, all of them intensely curious because they hadn't seen the inside of Pop-pop's house since the last time a man had run away from it. The women brought baked chicken and casseroles, like we were hosting a funeral. Jolie and I ate like pigs while the grownups talked in low voices. Occasionally people quarreled, and others hushed them or hurried them out of our earshot. There had never been such commotion, such numbers of visitors in Pop-pop's house. Relatives fed Jolie and me, petted us, fussed over us, but no one questioned us, no one ever asked what had happened, and as a result we never told.

Granny wielded guilt shamelessly during that first week. Later, after the excitement died down, the Hotvedts made themselves scarce, but for awhile Granny managed to get work out of them. The women cleaned for days, an exercise that fascinated me. The men repaired our back steps and put new packing and new washers in all the faucets. Granny complained that the trash barrel had rusted through, that we needed a new one. Our Hallsville uncle carried it away to the dump and made us another one out of a fertilizer drum. It smelled raw and stiff, like the granulated rat poison stored in Pop-pop's shed.

Granny harangued the men about the farmhouse. She fussed that Humphrey's abandoned place had become an eyesore and a danger to the children. It attracted vermin, maybe even tramps. Now that our daddy had run away there wasn't a man to board up the windows or chase away drifters.

Granny stayed in bed with her door closed the February day a bulldozer arrived and shoved the farmhouse over like it was Tinker Toys. Inside, Granny's things crashed and tipped and collapsed. Everything ground together like an accident in a combine.

The Hotvedts cleared out Daddy's feed store lending library. They gave away whatever books people would take. Miss Castle asked for the 1911 Britannica. The books nobody claimed got burned in a pit behind the store. I watched that fire, too, although we didn't need wood to help make it hot and white. The air above it quivered. Black ghost pages of ash would leap out of the fire as if trying to escape but already burnt beyond hope.

I never said a word about any of it, not even to Jolie, not even in my dreams. Still, the rumor happened that Jean Jouhaux had not run away, that he'd been killed and buried in the old farmhouse. The sheriff came from Columbia with his men and with a private contractor, and they pried up the ruins. They disentangled the smashed, gutted pieces of Humphrey's house, the inside walls of lath and plaster, the treads of narrow stairs, the glass shards from old-fashioned china trinkets. They dug down past the unshaken timbers. Most of the house had fallen into the cellar.

Jolie and I sat in our front yard, at the top of our hill, looking up the higher hill in front of us to where the men stood outlined against the April sky, to the crane as rigid and upright as a church steeple. It was Easter again, and we ate chocolate.

I said to Jolie, Do you think the Civil War man is in the cellar?

She shook her head, no. She said, He went away. But she never told me where, or how she knew.

In the end the sheriff found not one body but two, skeletons of murdered men dead a hundred years. Some remnant of a Confederate war widow's association took the remains for a proper soldier's burial after the university types made their examinations.

Granny went out of the house for the first time in years. She bullied Mom, who was recovered but frail, into taking her around town to church services, to the grocery store, to the cafe where we sat boldly at the window table. Granny grinned so her dirty teeth showed, grinned at every blessed soul in Sturgeon, Missouri, while Jolie and I sat open-mouthed, not thinking about it, each of us happy to get a piece of coconut cream pie. After Granny got her fill of showing up around town she retired for good to the unfinished house.

Mom lost her job a year later when she wore thin the pity of the car dealership owner. I guess we lived on welfare, but I'm not sure. Mom found work here and there. She was the nighttime companion for an old blind lady until the lady died. She did house-work and ironed twice a week for a university family in Columbia.

When I entered high school we got our telephone back because Mom needed it for a job that let her work at home. She made appointments for a baby photographer. On days when Mom felt sick I made the calls, and I remember being so surprised, so unsettled at how the housewives talked over the phone to me, gushy and sweet like I was one of them, like I might be a normal girl who would soon get a husband and my own baby to rock, to schedule portrait appointments for. They couldn't see me, and they didn't know me. They didn't know my family. They assumed I was entirely like them.

It was the first inkling I had that running away might make things different. I did run away. It made things different.

✤✤✤

I didn't know anything of my family until I turned thirty and realized I was strong enough and different enough to contact home. I took to writing letters four or six times a year and calling at Christmas. Granny had died. Mom had taken her place as the fat, old matriarch, although with a more benevolent rule. Jolie had married a man named Brad who won over the family and persuaded them to give him a lease on Pop-pop's original farm. He put beef cattle on the land, grew hay for winter feed, cultivated a vegetable crop that they harvested and canned and froze. Brad worked as a checker in a grocery store, and Jolie had hopes that he might make manager. The two of them belonged to the volunteer fire department. Brad was on call for emergencies, and Jolie ran the Wednesday night Bingo games.

Brad was handy, too. Jolie said he'd fixed most of the things in the house. They had a toilet. They had three kids.

When I turned forty I received a notice from a lawyer. My daddy had died. He'd been living in California, alone, and he left everything to me. His estate was nothing but books—books he'd acquired after having deserted us.

I could not have been more stunned if I had received a letter from Humphrey Hotvedt. Both men were ghosts long settled inside my soul, the secret mentors of my ambition, invisible sources of my passion. For a week deliveries of boxes arrived, like a spring flood. Boxes filled the floor of my apartment and stacked in towers around my table, my bed.

Running

THERE CAME a time when something interrupted Jack's run. It happened without warning and without pattern — irregular, unpredictable, shocking. Jack ran like a fish streaking through water when a shadow fell over him.

Jack Stuben ran daily when he could get away with it, when his body let him. He ran at four in the morning because at that silent hour the air smelled sharp and electric. He could be profoundly alone. There were no expectations, not even the burden of nodding to a fellow runner.

The shadow first touched him on a morning in early June, almost summer. The kids were not yet out of school. Jack broke stride and stopped. He shook as if some terrible crime had been committed on the trail in front of him. But nothing happened. Electric lights burned in the darkness, turning the air white, outlining individual leaves.

A week later the shadow hit him again. Jack did not stop. He stumbled and ran on. One moment he was generating heat off his skin like a furnace; the next moment his flesh turned crisp and cold. Adrenaline from a deep freeze saturated his blood. He tried to outrun the shadow. It crossed him briefly, wraithlike, but left a stone of fear. It troubled his sleep that night.

The shadow came for him again in two days. It disappeared for a week, then it spooked him three days in a row. He startled like a rabbit at noises.

Out of his fear there grew despair, small at first, like a rip in a long seam. It was barely visible. Jack refused to look at it because he didn't know how to mend it. The rent widened. If Jack had put his eye to it, to try and see what was on the other side, he would have found darkness without street lights, darkness as heavy and cold as the bottom of the ocean.

✿✿✿

The witch levitated twenty feet off the ground. From that height and angle the running trail looked like a black, sluggish river in an alien territory. Overgrown grasses, dense stands of bamboo, kudzu-infested trees covered its banks. Enormous, two-legged metal gridworks stood in single file, one giant every two hundred meters or so. Their outstretched arms carried high voltage electric lines. Buckled at the knee of each colossus was a photosensitive lamp that illuminated the trail at night, a discouragement against crime and vandalism. The swath of jungle ran for miles between the backyards of suburban homes. Forty years previously it had been a railroad track, but the trains stopped. The county bought the land, tore out the ties, paved a trail for running and biking. Vegetation on either side hid most of the tract houses. On high summer days, when runners sprinted along the blacktop, they felt hidden in a dusty green tunnel.

Jessica Freestone, a peculiarly suburban, nonrunning witch whose only exercise was mental flight, flew many times daily over the asphalt path behind her home. Fire and water were her only fears, so she carefully avoided the electric lines. She could not be seen. She did not cast a physical shadow because she was not physically there. Her mind drifted like a balloon, half asleep in the sun when she crossed the daytime runners. Recently she had become aware of Jack's four o'clock workout and made a special effort to see him, to cast over him her spectral shadow.

Reactions to Jessica's pall varied. Many runners left the trail. Some stopped completely, blaming their injuries. Others learned to avoid her section of the course, to detour along suburban streets. A persistent few, like Jack, continued. It never occurred to him to change his route, that the simple place or direction of his run might cause him grief. He could not afford to quit. Now that he'd turned forty-one, he considered with grim hilarity how old he had thought himself at thirty-five and at thirty-eight. The inevitability of the years impressed itself upon him, and running was all he knew of coping.

Jack had taken up running two years previously when his oldest child, then fourteen, joined the track team at school and began winning races. He attended her meets, as he had attended the sporting events of all his children, but the effect on him was different. Toni no longer seemed to be his daughter. Modestly clothed in shiny jersey and shorts, she became a nymph when she ran, a naked and alluring wood spirit, numinous, dangerous. He had to catch his breath and distance himself from her.

That spring he began to run. By August he had regained his wind, and he had learned to run early, before the heat. Early became earlier, until he was going to bed at nine or even eight-thirty in order to be up by four. Jack started to feel as if he had repossessed his body from some stagnant, deserted place, some place full of ruins, but his hold on it was tenuous.

"You run too much," his wife said. "It makes you tired."

Dianna was forever accusing him of being tired. Before the running, she had said, *You watch TV too much* or *You putter around the car too much* or *You play poker too much. It makes you tired.*

What she meant, he knew, had nothing to do with tiredness

but with a misuse of his energy. He lacked ambition. He'd worked the same job for fifteen years. He was content with it, aspired to nothing more. Jack was an engineer for the county, a building code inspector, a red tape man, an enforcer, a gadfly to contractors, to men who worked in the real world doing real things, producing things, making tangible, usable things. Jack liked his job.

So now, two years and two waist sizes later, Jack ran in spite of the flinch he'd developed on the trail. It was July, Friday, before dawn. A monotonous wind carried in a new weather front. The stars lay concealed behind black clouds that Jack could smell but could not see, clouds nearly bursting with rain. Droplets condensed on his skin like he was a glass of iced tea. Summer leaves exhaled in the wind, turned themselves so their undersides showed in the electric lights.

Out of that mute sky, as from a sleeve, came a woman's white hand. Jack thought of King Arthur and the enchanted hand that caught Excalibur. He ran faster. The hand descended from the cloud and pierced his chest with the long red nail of its index finger.

Bewilderment filled him. He stopped. Pain doubled him over. When he sat on the path it diminished. He felt at last only a keen sense of loss and abandonment. The rain fell on Jack for twenty minutes before he stood and walked home.

At the supper table that night Jack was very quiet. He'd agreed to make the salad, then he forgot to do it.

"You run too much," Dianna said. "It makes you tired."

"Can running make you hallucinate?" Jack said. "Can you feel hallucinations, or do you just see them? I thought they were visual."

Toni stopped eating and watched him with interest. The boys continued in their own world, poking each other and the dog.

"It depends on what you're drinking," Dianna said, trying for a joke.

"I think it matters how much imagination you have," Toni said.

Dianna looked with displeasure at her daughter, as though warning her to stay out of the exchange. Toni ignored her.

"Like in dreams," Toni said. "Some people have creative dreams and some people don't."

"I don't dream," Jack said, which was a bit of a lie.

"Yes, you do," Toni said. "You don't remember is all. I can tell you some ways to remember dreams."

"Maybe he doesn't have time to remember dreams," Dianna said. "Maybe he's busy earning a living so you can hang out with your friends and read dream books."

"Right," Toni said, "like I'm the champion hanger-outer. You don't know how good you've got it." Her face flushed with the effort of crossing her mother.

"Ryan threw his peas at me," said Ace.

"You dickhead," Ryan whispered.

Like a snake, Jack's hand leaped across the table and struck Ryan.

Silence ensued.

After awhile Toni resumed chewing, then said with her mouth full, "I thought you didn't hit. I thought it was against your religion or something."

Ryan began to cry. He was nine. Ace was seven.

"Well," Dianna said.

"Watch your mouth at the table," Jack said, deciding that he would not apologize. He wouldn't do it again, but he wouldn't apologize either. "Is there sugar in these vegetables?"

"Why?" Dianna asked.

"You know I don't want sugar in my food."

"It's a new recipe," Dianna said. "It's not much. We need variety. I need variety. I get sick of making the same things. Why am I explaining to you? Cook it yourself if you don't like it."

Her face grew rigid. Ryan was her favorite. Jack thought that Ryan acted sneaky and probably deserved what he got. Toni chewed like it was a profession, enjoying the conflict. Only Ace seemed unperturbed. He fed the disputed peas to the dog.

ቀ‑ቀ‑ቀ

Jack skipped his run Saturday and Sunday. Sleeping late was a luxury, and it put Dianna in a better mood. She always woke when his alarm went off at four. She specialized in sighing noises until she fell back into sleep.

Monday he ran again. The front had moved on and now there was no hint of rain. The predawn swelter lay wet and thick like a sleeping animal. Locusts screamed in the heat. Over their cries thrummed the drone of a thousand air conditioners.

The noise collected, condensed, became a booming sound that kept time with Jack's running feet. Again there were no stars, only a cover of blackness outside the grainy light of the street lamps. The humid air could not evaporate his sweat. The booming got louder. It sounded like an airplane except that it pulsed, at a pace faster now than his feet.

Jack slowed to a walk. He could hardly breathe the milky air. His sleeping neighbors, all those unknown competitors, the ones his wife wanted him to conquer although she never said so, dreamed their creative or not so creative dreams while he padded by them.

The booming grew outside and inside him. Something nearby, something above, disturbed the stillness. He looked straight up. Nothing. The booming matched the pounding of his heart. Both increased speed painfully. He breathed with it. He moved with it. The beat trapped him and squeezed him so he walked in a strobe light of sound.

When he passed the place of his vision he felt a dropping away in his heart. It was like suddenly falling in a dream.

Anxiety attack, Jack said to himself. He had read about such things. *It's death I'm afraid of*, he thought mockingly. Jack challenged death to show itself, to step into the channel of artificial light through which he ran. He commanded himself to jog with moderation. His heart knocked relentlessly. All the while he looked into the pools of darkness around trees, the dimness inside the tall, still grass. He looked for death like it might appear in a foreign film, hooded and cloaked and dancing with a scythe.

Jack made it home in that state, blinking like an idiot in time with the pounding noise. As he reached his driveway, the booming subsided and his breathing relaxed. There remained in the back of his head the sound of marching drums.

He dreamed it that night.

"My shoes hurt my feet," Jack told his wife the next day. "It gave me a hell of a headache. Never had anything quite like it."

Dianna picked up the shoes and looked at them. "How come all of a sudden?"

Jack shook his head.

At lunch he went to the shopping mall and bought a pair of two-hundred dollar shoes. He returned to his office, used the telephone to call an attorney and make an appointment. He was long overdue for drawing up a will. Dianna would be thrilled.

He looked at desk photos of his sons and thought how for them nothing existed prior to their childhood. All kids were that way. Jack had been that way. His own father lived most securely in Jack's memory as a tired, uniformed, delivery man, eternally forty-five years old, give or take a few. What it meant was that for Ryan and Ace, he, Jack, their father, was only now beginning to exist. This was the time on which they would anchor memories of him. The prior forty-one years were nothing, invisibility, smoke and mirrors.

Jack canceled his afternoon appointments and left work early.

It was a blistering day, white with haze. He would take the boys to the pool, maybe to a movie. He would try and convince Toni and Dianna to join them. Dianna worked as an aide in the school library so she and the kids had off all summer. Somehow Jack imagined the four of them sitting around the dim, air conditioned family room and drinking cold Pepsis. The boys would be at the computer. Toni would have a magazine. Dianna would be planning menus. She planned everything.

No one was home. The air conditioning roared. Lights burned everywhere. A TV upstairs chattered like there was a private party going on in a closed room. Only the dog greeted him, tongue out, oblivious to the unusual hour of his homecoming.

Jack had finished turning off things in the house when the front door slammed.

"Hey, Dad," Toni yelled. "You get fired?"

"You better hope not," Jack said.

She had a bulky, dark-headed girl with her. Both of them were wet and sleek as seals. They wore too-small bikini tops and too-large men's boxer shorts that hung so low the bottoms of their swim suits showed.

"We've been to the pool," Toni said unnecessarily. "We've got to change fast and get to work. Cindy's driving."

"Hi," Cindy said.

"Why are you home anyway?" Toni said. She seemed more polite than curious.

"Oh, I had the ridiculous notion I might spend some time with my family." Jack felt increasingly ridiculous as he said it.

"I think that's real nice," Cindy said.

"Sorry nobody's here to be with you," Toni said. "Gotta run."

Jack tried to remember where Toni worked. Once in mid-June he'd had to pick her up there and he knew the shopping center, but he couldn't recall if it was the Mexican restaurant or the ice cream place. Probably the ice cream shop. Toni was awfully young to have landed a real waitressing job. How would she serve the beer?

"Look on the calendar," Toni yelled from upstairs. "This is Tuesday so I think Ace and Ryan have karate. Then Mom drops them off for swim lessons and they stay for the team practice. Tuesday is her day to do volunteer stuff at the library. I know because sometimes she gets me to drive."

Near the end of this explanation, Toni came out of her door and walked leisurely toward the bathroom. Jack stood at the foot of the steps, in the family room. Its cathedral ceiling opened the view to the upstairs hallway. He got an eyeful of Toni in her underwear.

"For Christ sake, put some clothes on, Toni," Jack said. "You aren't a little kid."

Toni stopped and turned toward him. Her underpants were lacy and her bra was flesh colored. "Why?" she said, reasonably, conversationally. "I've got more on now than I do at the pool."

Jack decided it was wisest not to answer.

Instead of spending time with the boys he put his desk in order. Once Toni left, the house became silent and sheltering. He purged his files and consolidated the information on insurance policies. Fire and flood were Dianna's big worries. He threw away junk paper. He made a list of his assets and debts, a simple task. He made a list of everything Dianna should do if he died. She appreciated lists. Then he took out his book about investments and read three chapters.

✤✤✤

Jack suspended running that week.

"I need a rest," he told Dianna, who agreed.

He couldn't stop thinking about it. On days when he didn't run, gravity pulled like lead fishing sinkers in his muscles. His eyes and his skin itched.

On Saturday morning about eight he put on his bright new shoes, and he convinced Toni to run with him. First she had to dress right and fix her hair, in case anyone saw them.

"What a horrible day," she said to initiate their conversation on the trail. Not a hint of effort touched her face. She complained about everything, Jack thought, but they all did. It was a family habit. She looked fresh and bland and very, very young.

"What kind of day do you like?" Jack said. His breath was beginning to whistle in his throat but he could still be jaunty.

"I wish fall would come. It's too awful hot."

"The only summer of your life you'll be sixteen, and you're wishing it away."

"Oh, stop, Daddy," Toni said. "Life takes forever to go by."

Some unseen weakness afflicted his heart. Moist nostalgia haloed each leaf and grass blade, and Jack thought, *Remember this. Remember running with Toni.* He tried to look at everything at once.

"I don't like this place," Toni said. "How come nobody else is on this part of the trail? I've got the creeps."

"It is odd," Jack said, but he was washed over by sweet sentimentality. He thought his knees might buckle. He smelled fresh floor wax. The trees became green window shades rolled to let in the sunlight. He felt cared for. He would like to be a hermit, Jack thought, and live in a clean, bare room where time moved reluctantly. An unseen person brought him baskets of food that he forgot to eat. He studied old books.

"Dad, somebody's watching us," Toni said. "Do you think perverts hang around here?"

"Where?" Jack said.

Toni giggled and turned her head. "Over there. Look at the fat lady."

Face to face for only a moment, Jack saw her in the sky, not levitating, but in the flesh on her redwood deck, one corner of which jutted through the jungle to overlook the trail. She smiled intimately, not showing her teeth. Her right hand hung languidly over the rail, one red-tipped finger pointed toward his heart. She was enormous, overripe, burnished, her eyes like bruises in the fruity pulp of her face. She wore an old-fashioned muumuu, voluminous, ankle length, covered all over with large red flowers. She dyed her hair with henna. An oiled, burnt odor clung to her, as though she had flown too often, too near the sun.

Jack sighed. He ran on, his daughter ahead of him, a dream image. He looked instead into a room he'd forgotten where a small boy lay in a large bed made up with white cotton sheets, newly ironed. Jack had forgotten the sweetness of ironed sheets. The boy held a drawing board on his knees, and he busily, unself-consciously made pictures. He was perfectly happy.

"Dad, are you OK?" Toni said, dropping back with him.

Jack could not answer.

"Dad, you look like you're going to cry," Toni said, acting embarrassed. She glanced around for witnesses.

Jack stopped and panted. "It's too hot," he gasped. "You're right. I've got to stop running in this heat."

Toni guided him home, which he appreciated because he didn't feel capable of thinking. Dianna made him get into a cold bath and she rubbed his shoulders with alcohol.

"Do you know what happens when you have heat stroke?" she said. "Your brain swells. You go into a coma. You die." She started crying. "This time it's just heat exhaustion. You're sweating like a pig. That's how you know the difference. As long as you sweat you're OK. Remember that. Stop sweating and it's heat stroke. Promise me," Dianna pleaded, "next time you start seeing things, you'll stop."

Jack nodded.

"Go to a house. Any house. Get water. Drink it, and pour it on you. Lie down, and put your feet up."

Jack smiled. He loved Dianna for her lists, for her control. He wished he could ask her to buy white cotton sheets and to iron them daily, but it was a dream.

Dianna forbid him to run, at least, she said, until the heat wave broke. She could not stop his thinking about the fat woman, about her soft round hands.

At work Jack felt inert, clumsy, his timing off. He ran into flamers on the inspection sites, a contractor who went ballistic when Jack rejected some wiring and a homeowner who got in his face about a brother-in-law who was building an addition. Usually Jack defused anger or deflected it. Now he took it helplessly and the poison soaked him, soaked into him. His passivity triggered it, Jack thought, made it worse. He realized he'd been tired on the job for a long time. This was a cold, damp thought that stuck like wet paper to his heart.

Rain came, and fresh, new air from the north. Jack rolled out of bed with the four o'clock alarm. Still dim with sleep he pulled on his clothes, his new shoes. It was a ritual performed in the dark while Dianna rustled and sighed.

The breezy chill outside startled and delighted him. His flesh contracted, made goose bumps. He forgot to drink anything. Jack stretched and pulled and began to run, but, as on the job, he felt oddly listless, his body dormant. Energy had to be suctioned from deep inside him in order to keep the legs swinging in their familiar pattern. His legs were like machines, Jack thought, heavy and dull and impersonal, wanting only fuel to operate. On a good run all his parts responded to all his other parts, holding hands with each other and cheering him on. Sporadic running would ruin his conditioning.

Grim as a soldier, as desperate, Jack urged himself on. A yellow moon supported by two planets lay in the sky. A handful of the brightest stars pierced the electric light on the trail. The locusts sang slowly, sleepily. Jack's footfalls slapped the asphalt as regularly as a drum beat, then flew off into the black space that sealed itself around his tunnel of light. He ran through space. The path was a corridor—doorless, windowless, endless—taking him nowhere. Jack thought about cold water in a blue glass.

I'm crazy again, he thought. He trotted off the path. He bushwhacked through the weedy growth, the barricade of stiff greenery, and emerged in the neglected backyard of the witch. She watched him from an upstairs window as he circled the house, then she met him at the front door with his drink, as he had imagined, in a blue tumbler.

"Come in, dear," Jessica Freestone said. She wore a green gown that draped over the globular mass of her body, over the white, fruitlike flesh of her arms. She wore a ring on each manicured finger. Her henna-red hair swooped up in back and lipstick stained her teeth.

Jessica closed the door behind Jack, and he felt at once conflicting waves of peace and of great loss.

"I'm thinking of leaving my job," Jack said, amazed at his words. "And perhaps my wife."

His voice rang, as in a vacant house. The foyer looked bare and antiseptic. Jack followed the witch up half a flight of stairs to a long, unlit room, walled the entire length of one side with glass doors that opened onto the deck. Her house was like a ship, its deck railing the prow. From one end to the other Jack could see the tops of trees, gray in the reflected glow from the path. The moon dominated a black sky and cast the only illumination in the room.

The glass looked clean and brilliant. There were no drapes, no rugs on the freshly waxed floor. Nothing hung on the white walls.

A few pieces of furniture, wood and glass and chrome, gleamed, indistinct in the moonlight. As a frail, only child, Jack had been allergic to dust, and he had lived in such a bare house with his mother. His father had seemed like a visitor.

"You may stay here," Jessica said. The emptiness amplified her words.

She opened a door onto a white square room with a large white bed. Jack found his hot face pressed into the pillow, his mechanical legs afloat in white cotton, his entire self removed from the work of living. He felt cared for. He slept.

He woke in the same room, in the same cool bed. Someone had raised the green window shade and sunlight swept the floor. It was blond wood, highly waxed. Drawing board and paper lay on a chair by the bed. Disorderly stacks of books filled one nightstand. The other was made up for a sick room, with water and a thermometer and pill bottles. Jack remembered being six years old and having broken his leg. It mended poorly. He spent the long, long hours of summer in bed, reading and drawing. Drawing and reading.

"Stay with me," Jessica said, at his bedside. "Give up your running."

"But I like to run," Jack said. "It makes me feel young."

"You aren't young," she said. "You never will be."

Jack regretted having answered her. He needed to leave. His sick room looked spotless, forlorn and friendless as it had been that summer when his leg lay captive inside the cast. At times it had been unbearably hot and sticky and full of itches. He half expected his mother to walk in the doorway with a basket of fruit and sandwiches, with his foul medicine and the round silver spoon with which he had to drink it. But she didn't. His mother had been dead for six years.

"Jessica, Jessica!" a man's voice called. Someone's fist pounded on a door.

"My husband," Jessica said.

From her pocket she took a key ring, and she unlocked the door of the white room. She led Jack away from the bedroom, down, down the stairs to a hallway of closed doors. She chose another key, undid another lock.

"My husband likes to read," she said, opening on a room shelved wall to wall with antique, crumbling books. Six or seven lay, pages exposed, in a jumble on the floor. Others filled the seat of an easy chair.

A thin, round-shouldered man paced the floor inside the room. He held a book in one hand, a magnifying glass in the other. His face was full of fine wrinkles, as if it had been dried in a slow oven.

"Utterly fantastic," the man said. "Freshwater fish swell and blow up, KABOOM, unless they piss all the time. They never drink. You, young man," he said to Jack, although they were uncomfortably near the same age, "would never become thirsty if you ran nine hundred miles if you were a freshwater fish because to drink, to drink one drop, would be deadly. You would however be pissing constantly."

The man lay his magnifying glass in the book, used his free hand like a comb. He was freshly shaven, dressed in trim slacks and a short-sleeved button-down shirt, both of them stiff with ironed creases.

"Saltwater fish," he said, "on the other hand, have the opposite problem of, hear this, DEHYDRATION. 'Water, water everywhere, and not a drop to drink.' Ha! But they do drink. They drink saltwater because, do you know about osmosis? Of course you do. Every seventh-grader knows about osmosis. The fish have less salt in their bodies than there is in the ocean, so the ocean sucks water out through their skins. Amazing. And it's quite true. Here. Can you imagine drinking for your life, to save your life? Drink like a fish,

they say! Or piss like one. Which are you, freshwater fish or saltwater fish?"

"Do you run, sir?" Jack said.

The man had the gaunt, long-shinned look of a distance runner.

"Not any more," Jessica said.

"Fire and water," the man said with a wink. "You remember
that, young fellow. It's your only defense." He gestured toward
Jessica. "Fire and water are the only things that work on her, that
change her, like alchemy, like blood to bone. But wait, I just read
about blood to bone. Don't go away until I find it." The man threw
down his book and rifled in the pages of another, already open on
his chair. "Jessica, dear, you've seen fighters, boxers I mean, with
cauliflower ear. It's blood that got trapped when the poor bugger
got his ear smashed, but did you know it swells, and then it stays
there and by god it changes to cartilage."

"Such a baby," Jessica murmured. As her husband turned his
back she pushed Jack quietly out of the room, relocked the door.

"Who lives in the other rooms?" Jack said. He had an urge to
rush down the hall and put his ear to each chamber. He half
expected to hear the slap-slap of frustrated runners jogging in
place.

"The rest is private," Jessica said.

"I've had a very nice time," Jack said, like a boy leaving a bor-
ing party, "but I must go now. I enjoyed meeting you."

"You mustn't leave," Jessica said, her witchy eyes restless.
"There's nothing to outrun."

"Probably not," Jack said. All he'd done was ask for a glass of
water. There should be no obligation attached to that.

But again, he hadn't asked for the drink, Jack thought. The
witch had greeted him at the door with it. Did that make a difference?

Without looking or asking, Jack headed up the bare, blond wood stairs to the foyer. By the time he reached the door, he discovered he had only one shoe. His left leg was locked in plaster, a rigid exoskeleton like the shell of a beetle. He rattled the front door. It wouldn't open. He stumped up the stairs to the long, ship-like room, flooded with sunlight. His cast scratched the new wax, slipped on it. He felt his face and neck and realized that, even in panic, there was not a bead of sweat on him.

Heat stroke, for sure, he thought. *Dianna will kill me.*

"This is a very private place," Jessica said accusingly, as if he were an intruder. She climbed the stairs after him.

Only Dianna would be able to get him out, Jack thought. But she had carpools to run, committees to organize, children to chaperon.

If you want to come home, just come home, Dianna would say. *I can't stand all this hemming and hawing around. Make up your mind and stick with it.*

Too many people wanted too many things from him, Jack thought. He couldn't give up the running. If anything he needed to run faster.

Oh, phooey, Dianna's voice said in his ear. *What a lot of whining.*

Jack stared at the sliding glass doors to the deck. They distorted the sunshine, brilliant with color. Looking through them was like being at the bottom of a clear sea and gazing up through the water to the surface. Beyond it hung the sky, made alien by distance and by the refraction of light.

"Rest now," Jessica said. She filled her mouth with chocolate, offered Jack some from a frilly box. "Go to your room now."

"I don't know where it is," Jack said. He heard himself whine, and he cringed. In his mind, he saw Dianna look annoyed.

"Of course you know where it is," Jessica said. "You grew up here." Her hand holding the key ring pointed to a closed door.

"But I'm not sure," Jack said.

"Of course you're sure." Jessica seemed less patient. She flowed in the green dress across the bare floor. She opened the door to the square, white room.

Jack felt his overheated brain swell, like the freshwater fish. He stumped his way toward her. "I don't understand," he said. "You have to show me."

Jessica sighed. She turned and stepped inside the room. "It's all here, every blessed thing you remember and a few things you don't."

Now or never, Jack, Dianna's cool voice said.

He reached out and plucked the key ring from Jessica Freestone's hand, deftly and surgically, as one would snatch a dangerous object from a toddler. He gave her a tremendous shove. His hands sank into her flesh as though it would collapse around his wrists, but she tottered at last. She shrieked without dignity. Jack slammed the door. It had a deadbolt lock that he turned.

"Now what do I do?" Jack said aloud, but Dianna gave him no more advice.

Jessica hammered on the other side of the bedroom door.

Fire or water, Jack thought, were his only defense. Fire seemed too drastic, too criminal, but water he could do. He went from kitchen to bathroom to bathroom, turning on the taps, plugging the drains. He struggled down the stairs to the hallway of locked doors. He beat on each one of them, yelled, tried keys in the locks. No one answered. The few rooms he opened were stale and vacant. Jack's voice clattered in the emptiness. The only other sound he heard was that of gushing water.

How to get away. *Just come home,* Dianna had said.

He tried the front entrance again, but the deadbolt locked with a key not on Jessica's ring. He stumped back up to the long room, studied the sliding glass doors to the deck, tugged at them. The outside sky seemed to have retreated further beyond the oceanlike atmosphere. The sun looked smaller.

Malevolent magic, Jack thought. The house had been changed by the witch, had become a glass boat sunk deeply in the sea.

"You mustn't open the doors," Jessica shouted from the white room.

"Why not?" he murmured, but he knew. Here was all the water in the world. Before he could take time to think about it, Jack used his club of a plaster cast to smash the plate glass doors.

"Now you've done it!" Jessica wailed.

A powerful wave, a mad surge of water sprayed Jack across the floor and slammed him against the opposite wall. The cast shattered. After the first impact he shook his head, then watched as the room flooded. He knew that once the water level rose above the hole in the glass, he would simply dive under and swim through it, stroke his way past the redwood deck, across the ill-kempt yard, surface, and body surf through the tops of the trees until the waves returned him to the running trail.

That was what he did. Jessica called to him once before the deep water obliterated her voice. Wisely, Jack did not look back.

When he reached home, on foot like any mortal, Jack discovered he had lost one of his new shoes.

❖❖❖

They were in bed with the lights out when Dianna said, "Are you having an affair?"

"No," Jack said, his face flushed.

"You sound awfully damn guilty," Dianna said.

"I think about things," Jack said. "It shakes me up. I think about leaving my job."

"That might not be such a bad thing," Dianna said. "Do you

think about leaving us?"

Us, Jack thought. *Us, instead of me.*

"Sometimes," he said. "I don't think about actually doing it. I think about what it would be like, how things would be different."

Dianna cried in the darkness.

"It's very confusing," he said. "I plan to stay, but I think about leaving. I went in this lady's house today, to get a drink of water like you warned me to do, and I saw how they lived. I can't explain it. It was just a house, like all the other houses, but I went in and she brought me this glass of water, and I felt like the place was a boat in the middle of the ocean, and they were all waiting to drown."

"Liar," Dianna said. "You're going to leave."

"No," he said, confident then of his answer. "No, I'm not. It's just a game, the thinking. It's just a way of pretending, like make-believe, like Toni used to do make-believe and dress-up when she was little, before the boys came."

After Life

THE GUN was gone and so, logically, should have been most of her own head. Terrianne's first thought concerned her appearance. She used her fingers to explore face, hairline, the high crown of her scalp. Heat evaporated off skin like something tangible, like vapor, but there seemed to be no evidence of her crime.

Oh, hell, she thought, I'm a ghost.

It was night. Terrianne stood in the snow as she last remembered, by the fallen cottonwood. The tree had been a monster. Its collapse several years before opened a clearing in the woods where wild azalea and a few light-starved dogwood struggled. Maple and oak seedlings invaded the ground. Each miniature tree, each branchlet and twig, stood separate and apart, sealed with its own perfect silhouette of snow.

The snow lay shallow and fresh and wet, without a shadow. Light radiated democratically. The impersonal light saturated the air.

Terrianne had walked into the woods shortly after midnight. The sky was black, but she had not needed a lantern. She had brought only the gun, its clip fixed inside, like a stone in the cargo pocket of her parka. She had come to the woods because she believed, or had believed, that the mystery was in the trees.

Oddly, Terrianne realized, she did not believe anything now, not one way or the other. She had feelings but they were more the memory of feelings, and they too seemed to be evaporating, carried off by the steam of her body heat.

I'll freeze solid if they don't find me, Terrianne thought.

She wondered how that would affect her and then forgot to think about it. Without surprise Terrianne became aware that the gun lay across her two open hands.

There is a name for it, she thought.

It was blue-black and oiled. The barrel and the stock made a severe, obtuse angle where they joined, and out of the intersection came the silver tongue of the trigger. It was a Ruger, a precise gun, a rifled .22 full of hollow-point bullets. Even as the names materialized, she forgot them.

Terrianne forgot the gun. In her hands lay a hard-skinned reptile, so still it seemed enchanted. Its silver tongue sucked the remaining warmth from her fingers. In another time she had been told that cold did not exist, only the absence of heat. She stood as motionless as the reptile, content with stillness. The last of her body heat fled inside to her heart and lungs and liver, where it hid, silent and insulated.

The mystery is in the trees, Terrianne thought.

She saw in the tree trunks around her the serene and featureless faces of the dead. They had no eyes or mouths. Their arms, gloved in snow, reached above them. To join these dead was a homecoming.

I have never been depressed, Terrianne thought. I have been homesick for the other side.

Inexplicably, the thought triggered a rebellion. Terrianne had to walk. She could not bear the root-like way she was sinking into the ground. She traveled without design, her boots scooping the wet snow. She maneuvered around and under things, prickly brambles and branches and deadfalls, all of them made complicated by snow. The false light lay close to the land. The sky was black. Nothing cast a shadow.

Step by step, Terrianne watched her boots plow into and lift the snow. The step by step rhythm, one after the other after the other, became suddenly important, although Terrianne could not remember why. She could not remember the name for the bright color of her bootlaces. They were clever boots, fake fur with black rubber soles. Terrianne stopped and took them off, first the right, then the left, and stood in her bright stockings, the same forgotten color as the laces.

They are such nice boots, Terrianne thought. I'd like to keep them.

She leaned against a tree and pulled off her socks by their toes. Wet and brittle, the stockings came loose reluctantly.

Nothing here is made, Terrianne thought.

She took off her parka and examined it, along the double turned seams and the enormous zipper, admired what intelligence had made it. Nothing was made in the land of the dead. There was no step by step time in which to make it. Regretfully she lay the coat on top of the boots, then forgot them both.

Carefully, deliberately, Terrianne removed her clothing—her jeans, her Shaker knit sweater, her thermal undershirt trimmed in ribbon, her cotton panties with the clean panty shield. She concentrated on the order in which she removed things, whispering the sequence as if in a party game. It seemed terribly important that the sweater came after the jeans and before the undershirt. The sweater itself was terribly important, Terrianne thought, using her finger to trace how it was made stitch by stitch from a single line of yarn. She was jealous of the sweater, jealous of how it could be made stitch by stitch, step by step.

This is the same jealousy felt by the gods, Terrianne thought, jealous and unforgiving as they are to the living.

She walked, naked and white and shining like a candle. She forgot her name and the names of the trees. She forgot how she came to the woods. She walked until she forgot she was walking, until she was near to giving herself to the trees, until she looked down at an unrecognizable figure, bloody in the snow.

She knelt and dipped her fingers in the cold blood, as thick and black as hard candy. She put one finger in her mouth. The winter woods vanished. Summer burst upon her—trees bathed in hot green leaves and dust, sunlight in mottled waves, leaf mold with her footsteps through it. She smelled something like fire high in her nostrils, something vibrant and hot with flesh on it.

The moment retreated, ended.

Greedily she smeared blood on her hand and put all four fingers in her mouth. A memory exploded through her. She drove her old car, the Datsun, the one she called The Bucket, drove it on some damaged road where the small, hard tires collided with potholes and gravel. Sweet, hot anger filled her. She did not know why. She gripped the steering wheel so it imprinted her palms. Its plastic cover with the unraveled lacing moved like loose skin. Sweat sealed her shirt to the vinyl seat back. Her jeans chafed. A residue of cigarette smoke filmed the inside of the windshield. Permeating everything was the exuberant, juice-filled energy of her anger.

The dream ended. She could not remember the dream or where it came from or why it held her so fiercely. All she knew was the troubling unfairness of it, like homesickness for a place she could not remember. She put both hands in the blood.

Mr. & Mrs. Tattoo at the Amusement Park

You're eleven, you're a girl, it's summer, & all you want is to be normal, part of a normal family that's normal in the right way. The right way is crucial. There's normal & there's not-normal, & while you can't list the criteria for either, you know it when you see it. Families either come like families are supposed to be, normal, or they don't.

Your family might make it. Mom teaches the after-school religion class called CCD. On one hand it's embarrassing, but on the other, she knows a lot of the right kids & can gossip about them. You are glad that you go to public school, even if it means the extra class on Wednesday afternoons. Dad coaches wrestling at St. Luke, the parochial high school where big brother Paul goes. Paul is highly intelligent according to everyone, but not working up to his potential. You consider him a turd. Big sister Trish is merely a pill. She acts stupid as a brick & probably is. You are the unknown quantity, even to yourself. Little sister Cathy is in kindergarten & doesn't count yet.

This family takes a vacation trip that, in your mind, becomes a kind of normalcy test. It's a trip to HersheyPark, the kitschy Chocolate World amusement park in Hershey, Pennsylvania. Your family's been on plenty of low-budget trips before, but this one's different, in a way you regret without realizing that you do. You seem to remember an earlier time when all of you had effortless fun, but you can't say when it was.

At the park, you observe the crowd mercilessly. You look for black socks with the wrong kind of shoes, for unacceptably gross sunglasses, for unwaxed thighs exposed by summer shorts, for bad hair. You analyze in an instant which families make it & which families don't. Most don't & you dismiss them. You measure your own family as it wavers into & out of the acceptable range.

What you don't know & can't know is that this amusement park trip is as good as it gets. Before next year, Daddy will have his accident. He'll get smashed up in the car & go live in a rehab ward, where the nurse shaves his face every day with something that leaves his skin damp & rubbery & smelling like cherry candy.

But that is the unknown, in the future. Right now the brilliant sheen of summer light allows no secrets. Your family walks among the outdoor, primary colors of trees & sky & tall signs, of striped pavilions, souvenir shops, & the fortress-like scaffolding for roller coasters. The hot pavement burns through your soles, right up into your ankles. The sun burns the tips of your short hair, your round, brown shoulders. You smell suntan lotion & pink sugar cotton candy & chlorinated water. The low, cranking drone of machinery & the higher pitched wail of voices saturates the air with noise. People surround you—people on benches, people in canopied lines, people drinking & discussing & swooshing through the sky in metal gondolas—all of them aligned, it seems, in families.

You see, perhaps for the first time, how your own family is stamped with a look-alike brand.

Paul sulks. He walks skinny & slouched over, his shirttail out, hands driven deep in the pockets of his shorts. He presses his lips shut in a sour expression, & in response Daddy is pressing his own lips shut in exactly the same way. Daddy doesn't shave as often as Mom wants him to. It makes his jaw look dark & scary.

"Oh, the swings!" Mom says in her make-happy voice. "They are my favorite ride. We have to go on them." She jostles little Cathy's arm like it might perk her up. Cathy's been fussing about wanting a grape drink.

"Big whoop," you hear Trish say kind of low & sneaky.

You see Mom's white bra strap looping out from the armhole of her sleeveless blouse. You think how the tops of her arms are baggy. Trish's bare arms & yours & little Cathy's are sleek.

"We have to go on the swings," Mom says again. "I remember a time, the summer after high school, when my best girlfriend & I went to the fair & we rode on the swings a hundred times." She's going to tell you about it now. She's gearing up for it.

Daddy says, "Let's go on the swings for your mother," & you think it's because he wants to cut her off.

You get in a line that has no wait at all. You are at the park on a Monday, on purpose, so the crowds will not be bad. The ride is called the Wave Swinger, & when the attendant lets down the gate your family surges with the others, each rider claiming a bucket seat swing that hangs by long chains from the ornate, carousel-style roof. You buckle in. The structure begins to turn & your family calls to one another, makes faces & hand signals. The swings rise into the whistling air. Bare legs dangle in pairs off each one. Even Paul forgets to act sullen. He stretches out his arms as if to glide, & you copy him. You watch the swings lift & separate & skim the leaves of nearby trees, & you know this must be close to flying.

The line is so short that as soon as the ride ends your family hurries through the exit & back to the entrance & right back into their empty swings, never missing a turn. You do that once, twice, then on the third time a delay happens.

Paul starts twisting around & frowning. You hate that because when Paul gets angry, then Daddy gets angry & yells about respect. Then Mom pretends there's no conflict going on, & Trish yells at Mom for pretending. Cathy misses the whole thing, she's such a space shot. You are the one who suffers. You are suffering already & the hubbub hasn't even started.

You wait until you figure out that everything is stopped so this wheelchair guy can be put on a swing. He's kind of spastic, but not too bad. He doesn't drool. His head is over to the side & one arm doubles up next to his shoulder. He leans some, but he doesn't jerk. One of the HersheyPark people wheels him to a swing, lifts him into it like he's a big baby. You can't believe it. You wonder if he will fall out, & then won't everybody be upset.

Finally the swings begin to move. That's when you see the Tattoo family, only at a distance you don't see their tattoos yet. You see instead their strange white faces, their black hair that bushes out in ponytails & mustaches & beards & eyebrows. The Tattoo people stand in the shade near the trees & eat ice cream. They look to you like they eat a lot of ice cream. They point & wave to the wheelchair man & laugh from the pit of their big bellies.

You find it shocking, almost as shocking as the wheelchair man himself.

The swings lift you as tenderly as the hand of God. You let go of earthly things & let the hand pull you out & up until it's just you, on your own, towed up into the sky & set free. You put your arms out like wings. The air rushes to meet you, slides past you, on & on, air that never ends. Your hair streaks behind you. Your shorts puff up with wind. Leaves & sky & leaves again charge at your face, then dash away.

You soar alongside the wheelchair man. He sits crookedly, rigid as a pole. You think about how he can't move, & yet here he is, flying. You feel proud to be on the ride with him, chasing the same air with him. He puts out his good arm like he's a little boy, & he becomes just like you, like your family. You wish right then that the chains of his swing will come free & he will keep going higher. All your swings, your family's swings, will break loose, & you will follow him. There will be a flock of you in the sky, beating your wings & calling to each other.

❀❀❀

Your family's mood is improved after the swings. Mom & Daddy announce that after lunch they will let Paul & Trish go off for two hours on their own. They say you can go, too, but you say no, you'll stay with Cathy. Paul & Trish do stuff that scares you, roller coasters & things.

Trish is so excited she's vibrating.

Daddy says, "I wish I could always make you so happy."

Trish doesn't get it, & you don't either.

First you all go on a family ride, a water ride called the Canyon River Rapids. There's a forty-minute wait during which Mom embarrasses the crap out of you kids by insisting you put on more sunblock lotion & by pulling Baggies of cut up apples & carrots out of her monster purse.

It turns out you have something interesting to study while you ignore Mom. You get your first real look at the Tattoo people. They stand in line ahead of your family, but because the line snakes through a maze of metal fences, there are times when you stand side-by-side with them. You stare. You figure it serves them right, considering how they acted toward the wheelchair man & how they must be advertising for attention, covered all over like they are with naked fairies & mermaids & roses & doves.

Even they travel as a family. There's Mr. & Mrs. Tattoo, & another man who looks like he might be Uncle Tattoo. They have an almost grown girl who looks normal but seems to fit in with them, & two boys near your age who are totally weird, the kind of boys you feel sorry for but you avoid because kids are mean to you if you have anything to do with them. The whole family wears tank tops & floppy shorts & thick leather sandals. The normal girl has a moon on her ankle. You see skulls on the upper arms of the boys, but you're pretty sure they are temporary tattoos, the kind you buy in packages at the drugstore.

It's the grownups who are spectacles. They all three have shoulders like buffalo & black hair in their armpits, even the mother. They have bloated stomachs & flat butts & great big thighs like sausages decorated with rocket ships & dragons. Their meaty arms are twined about with fruit & flowers & nude women. You see a blue knight on Mr. Tattoo & a bleeding heart on the Missus Uncle Tattoo sports a picture of a lady holding a sword & a crisscross of barbed wire.

You gaze at the green snakes on the Tattoo family until you are hypnotized. You are locked inside this swaying, sweaty crowd of people. Your clothes never feel comfortable anymore, tight & loose in all the wrong places, hot against your skin. Up above the canopy, the blue sky goes on forever, & you listen to the private chatter around you.

A final twist in the line reveals Mr. Tattoo standing behind Mrs. Tattoo, his hands on her shoulders in an intimate, casual way, like he might be giving her a neck rub, but he is *bumping* her.

You see nothing but the two of them. Mr. Tattoo swings his bottom half, from his waist to his knees, so he bumps his private parts against Mrs. Tattoo's rear end.

You think you will have a heart attack.

Mrs. Tattoo looks lazily over her shoulder at him, but she doesn't act particularly alarmed. He bumps her a couple more times, & that is when you get a picture in your head of dogs doing it. You turn sweaty & red. Trish says she thinks about stuff like that, but you don't. You aren't used to it.

Then the Tattoo family is on the final stairway down to the dock. They move like a herd through the red-shirted attendants. They board their raft with much noisy talk about who sits where, & they whisk away on the fake river.

"Hey, cool, you can buy a video," Trish says. She shows you a sign that announces how cameras are set up along the route.

"What a snore," Paul says.

"I think it's clever," Mom says. "We can wave at the cameras."

You see people climbing stairs from the other side of the dock. They are coming off the ride. They smile & wring out their wet T-shirts, flap their shirts in the hot air, shake their sodden hair. You look to them for clues about how the ride will be.

Then you've waited & waited & it's your turn. You watch what the people in front of you do so you can memorize it & copy exactly the right thing so you can be prompt & helpful to the college kids running the ride. You don't want them to think you're an idiot who doesn't know how to buckle whatever belt or bar holds you in. You want them to notice how clever & quick you are, how you pay attention & know what to do. It works this time, & a cute guy winks at you.

You get into the raft. It's shaped like an enormous tire & there are six seats, just the right number. Your family sits down right away, not fussing & switching places like the Tattoo family.

"No life jackets?" Daddy says. "What if we capsize?"

"What's capsize?" you say, imagining something dangerous.

"Oh, Daddy," Trish says, "these things never capsize."

He pretends to be skeptical.

"What's capsize?" you say.

"There's the first camera," Mom says. "Wave, kids."

You bounce & wave. Trish laughs her self-conscious monkey laugh. Paul makes faces. He's hit by a water spout.

"What's capsize?" you say.

Your raft twirls around in the fake rapids. Cathy screams so Daddy will let her sit in his lap, then when the waterfall comes they both get drenched. Cathy hunkers over, trying to make herself small, but the water pours coldly over her. Daddy lies back & spreads out his arms. He looks ready to hug that waterfall, or to grab it & pull it into the boat. The water casts itself into the sky as mist, as white spray, as something not solid or liquid, & not yet ready to be air.

The final waterfall soaks your entire family. Mom bows her body over her monster purse, protecting the first aid equipment inside. She laughs while streams of water run from her hair into her eyes. Mom doesn't wear make-up. Trish does, sooty black, but it's waterproof.

Then your raft stops floating. You are on a conveyor belt that trundles your party to the finish point. Now it is your turn to walk, smiling & dripping, past the hot, bored line of people, all of them looking to you for clues about the ride. You do your part to act bright & splendid with happiness so they will know the wait is worth it.

You leave by wooden stairs that take you first up & then down into a cabana-like shelter where a high-tech wall of monitors plays videos of the river ride. Clutches of wet people stand near the screens & watch themselves.

"That's us," Trish says, always the alert one.

She points to the top, right screen. The movie is just beginning, & your family is still dry. Daddy gives you a quick pat on the knee. How could you have forgotten that? Seeing it in the video brings it back, but not like the real pat. It feels like you have acquired a memory. The whole video is like that. It isn't your memory of the ride. You re-experience Cathy's round mouth when she screams & Paul's snotty attempts at humor & Trish's exaggerated laugh. You see for the first time how Daddy embraces the waterfall.

You had your arms over your head the first time it happened. Now you see it on video & it becomes your memory of the waterfall. It replaces your other memory.

"I want to buy it," you say.

Everybody looks at you with interest & new respect.

You see a sign that says nine dollars for the video. That sounds reasonable. Mom is holding your spending money.

"I'd like to purchase that," you say rather formally.

Paul grabs your arm & steers you out of the cabana while Mom & Daddy discuss the situation.

"You can't get it," Paul says into your ear.

"I like it," I say. "I want it. I have my own money."

"You can't get it," he says urgently. "I gave it the finger. It's on the tape."

"That's your problem," you say, so bold you can't believe it. You feel good. "That's your problem. Live with it."

"You'll pay," Paul says, & he gives you an arm burn.

"Paul's hurting me," you holler.

He lets go. You run back into the shelter, right up to the counter where a blond-headed girl sits on a stool & twirls her hair around her finger.

"Number 22," you say. "I want the video that was on 22."

"Check with your parents," the girl says, barely looking at you.

Mom tunnels through the contents of her bag—packets of crackers, tea bags, extra tissues & moist towelettes, insurance cards, chains of safety pins—to locate your coin purse. You count out the dollar bills, then the quarters, & finally you get down to dimes before you have enough money. This takes time. Mom & Dad stand patiently by. Cathy whines. Paul stomps off in a fury. Trish acts mortified. She has to walk away & pretend she isn't part of the family. You don't care. She never gets embarrassed when you stand around waiting for *her* to do some terribly important thing like choose a fingernail polish color at the drugstore.

Then it's done, & you're all famished. You go to Taco Bell & sit at an outdoor table that you cover with drink cups & paper wrappings. Unfortunately, the Bizzy Bees kiddie ride is nearby. It makes an annoying racket, & as a result nobody talks. You think that's kind of nice. You get to snarf down your tacos & stare off into the distance until you realize that you are staring at them again, the Tattoo family, as big as life, munching away on burritos.

You look straight into the faces of Mr. & Mrs. Tattoo & you think, *They look like twins.* They even chew alike, sideways instead of up & down, never quite closing their mouths. They both have black eyebrows that meet over their noses. They both have black hair that reaches halfway down their backs, Mr. Tattoo's in a sleek ponytail & Mrs. Tattoo's in a rumpled braid.

You think that maybe they have exchanged parts of themselves with each other, because she is a woman who looks kind of like a guy, & he's a guy who looks kind of womanish. Mrs. Tattoo is tough. You can imagine her on a motorcycle or breaking a chair over someone's head. Mr. Tattoo is soft, marshmallowy. He has a bold mustache & an itty, bitty beard that he trims in a fancy shape. He holds his hands delicately, like he's at a tea party.

They see you.

First, Mrs. Tattoo hits one of her boys when he reaches across the table. She just smacks him upside the head without warning. The boy holds his ear, but he doesn't cry, & he snags the thing he was reaching for. Uncle Tattoo, who wears his beard in two Viking-like braids, cracks some kind of joke, because they all bust out laughing, spurting burrito in the air. That's when Mrs. Tattoo nudges her husband & points at you.

You realize you must look like a real dummy, staring at them with your eyes bugged out. The whole Tattoo family grins & waves.

You look down quickly & cram the rest of the taco in your

mouth so you have to chew with your cheeks puffed out. Trish would die a thousand deaths before she would let weird people wave to her.

You decide right then that you aren't going to be like Trish & be embarrassed by everything, like the whole world isn't good enough for you. You look up, chipmunk-like, furiously chewing the taco, & you wave back.

They like it!

They smile in a friendly way, like normal people, like anybody would, then they return to their jokes & their burritos, & you know it's time to stop watching them. Here you thought they were so rude to the wheelchair guy, & you were doing the same thing. In fact, maybe they weren't laughing at him. Maybe they were smiling & waving to him just like they did to you. The more you consider it, the more possible it seems.

After lunch Paul & Trish go off on their own. They talk Mom & Daddy into three hours instead of two, & they rush away like rats let out of a cage. You see how Mom & Daddy relax about one hundred fifty percent with them gone. Cathy stops being so whiny. The four of you troop around to things like the Tilt-A-Whirl & the Skyview & Dry Gulch Railroad.

Everywhere you go, sooner or later, the Tattoo family is there. It's like when you learn a new word & suddenly everywhere you look, there's the word, & you'd swear that before it had never existed. That's how the Tattoos are. The second they appear any-where near you, *bam*, you see them. They pop right out of the crowd.

You wave when you see them, & they wave back. Mr. Tattoo slaps his forehead & acts amazed. How could you meet again so soon? Mrs. Tattoo play punches him. The boys pull on their ears & make faces, but you already knew they were strange.

Mom & Daddy & Cathy never notice this ritual. It's like you've found a window into a new part of the world, a secret, exotic piece of the world unknown to the rest of your family. You are made dizzy by your exclusive knowledge.

✧✧✧

The last time you see Mr. & Mrs. Tattoo, you get the closest to them. It's while standing in line again, of course. Even on a Monday, waiting seems to be a major part of the day.

You & Cathy & Mom & Dad are going on the Coal Cracker, a flume ride with one dreadful plunge straight down that makes your stomach balloon into your chest, that makes your skin sting all over, that lifts you off the seat just enough to convince you that you are going to fall, fall, fall. A camera clicks your picture halfway down.

The fourth or fifth time you get in line, there stand the Tattoos again, in front of you, not right in front, but close enough that you hear them talking. They talk loudly so you can't miss it.

"You all gotta scream so it shows in the picture," one of the boys says.

"You see me scream all day," Mrs. Tattoo replies lazily.

"We're gonna buy a picture. We got our own money," the other boy says.

The almost grown girl snorts. "That is so stupid. I'll scream if I want to scream, not for some old picture."

"Your mama comes by it natural," Uncle Tattoo says, "screaming I mean. Your grandpa was a champion hog-caller for the Tri-State area back home."

"What's Tri-State?" asks one of the boys.

"What's tricycle?" Mr. Tattoo says. "What's triangle? What's triceratops?"

"Try it. You'll like it," Mrs. Tattoo says.

"I will." Mr. Tattoo leans forward & bites her shoulder.

"But what is it?" the boy persists.

Then they are gone, pushed ahead into the boarding area. It must be ninety degrees right then, without a breath of wind, but goose flesh rises up on your arms & on the back of your neck. You shiver inside so it squeezes your heart. You can't see things clearly—there's too much color, too many things moving, too many people talking. Your skin is like a box locking you inside it.

You lean against Mom & she puts her arm around you, rubs her hand up & down so the shivering stops. She thinks you are bored.

"Getting tired of this ride, honey?" she says.

You are afraid you might cry. A terrible feeling grips you, that you are no different, no more special than any other kid in all of HersheyPark.

They are just like us, you think.

The Tattoo family is just like your family.

You stand where you can see the Tattoos get into their long, log-shaped car. It is a tight fit, but they all six make it. These cars don't have separate seats, just one bench down the middle, & you put your legs on either side of it. When you lean back, you lean back into the person behind you. The Tattoos look pretty cozy in there, touching front to back, shouting at each other.

Their car glides to a ramp where, with a click, clack, click, it is hauled up an incline to the beginning of a sluice. The incline is perilously steep. People sitting in the front of the car have to pull forward or they squash the people behind them.

You see the Tattoo family, their car halfway up the ramp, when the entire Coal Cracker flume ride breaks, quits, stops cold. The electrical power vanishes & with it goes every piece of machinery—motors, winches, pumps, radios, security systems, ventilation fans, the whole works. You hear the calm & surprising sound of running water. It's been there all along, unnoticed, rushing silkily beneath the mechanical noises.

The red-shirted college kids stop loading people into cars. They yell into walkie-talkies. Out on the ride itself, a girl climbs ladders you've never noticed before. She stops & shouts something to the Tattoo family. The six heads in their car are twisting & turning. Arms wave. Bodies move sideways. They are far enough away that all together they look like one squirmy bug stuck on a spider web.

"What do you think happened?" Mom says to Dad.

Your family leans on a railing that gives a good view of the stranded car.

"I don't know," Daddy says. "Maybe there's a weirdness-meter. When people who are too weird go through, it trips the meter & stops the ride."

Mom & Daddy act like this is their own hilarious & long-running joke.

You realize they have seen your Tattoo people all along.

But they haven't really.

❀❀❀

A year later, it's summer again, but you won't be taking any trips. The accident is now history, & you are adjusting to the permanent, non-normal status of your family. You wake up one night, & you just have a feeling. You go down to the family room, & you find Paul, eternally sullen, running the Canyon River Rapids video over & over. You watch with him. Paul shows you where he really did flip the bird at the camera, but in so cowardly a way you have to know to look for it.

Before the accident happens, during the months in between your family trip & Daddy's car crash, there is a brief time when this video becomes your memory of HersheyPark. On your own, you forget about the family quarrels & the wheelchair man's flight &

the Tattoo family in limbo.

Then your daddy is hurt. Somewhere in the confusion of the following hours you look back. Time rearranges itself, & you give up the present moment in order to revisit, minute by minute, that hot, bright vacation day. It is a sudden & vibrant memory, as if a probe has stimulated the corner of your brain where it is stored.

You see your final image of the Tattoo family, eternally scrambling inside their little car, heaving themselves forward so as not to crush Uncle Tattoo at the bottom, looking around boldly, fearlessly for the spider in whose web they are caught.

The Wine of
Astonishment

I

Mr. Murdoch, a member of
our church, came to dinner once at my parents' house. "And what
do you do?" he asked me in the benign way of adults.

"I fly," I said, self-righteously.

My parents hid their discomfort, and Mr. Murdoch said, "Do
you really, now?"

Without moving my chair I flew directly up from the dinner
table, turned a triple somersault and ended with an arabesque over
the pot roast.

"You did mention her flying," Mr. Murdoch said to my mother.

I spun like an ice skater over their heads. My mother looked
with consternation at the dining room light, which I was in danger
of hitting.

"What else does she do?" Mr. Murdoch asked.

"Not much," my father admitted.

"If she ever needs employment," Mr. Murdoch said, "once
she's out of school, I mean, then send her to my company. The
Agency takes on flyers, and I guarantee her a job."

My parents accepted his business card, returned his professional handshake, and thanked him with an intensity I found

embarrassing. I wondered at the fuss. I knew what an outrageously good flyer I was. I anticipated more out of life than employment.

✢✢✢

I did not think of Mr. Murdoch's offer until eight years later, when I left college without graduating. In fact, I left three different schools. I had become unpopular for flying during class, floating rather, at window level when possible and imagining my own feats in the bright broad daylight skies. Those who were kind smiled indulgently, and I learned to feel shame.

It could not last, so I scheduled an interview at The Agency and was presented to Ms. P. Danaan, an intimidatingly elegant woman of early middle age. She anchored her hair with silver combs. Her face was so white the blood from it seemed to have drained into her painted lips.

Ms. Danaan smiled at me with wonderful intelligence. I wanted very much for her to understand the sincerity of my flying. I leaped up toward the ceiling to perform a handspring off the acoustical tiles, only to discover they were not fastened but lay suspended on a metal gridwork. Tiles tumbled up into the dark dead space above, the space for furnace ducting and electrical cables. Two tiles broke. They shattered dust over my hair and rained pieces of plaster onto the teak desk. I hovered over Ms. Danaan, my arms buried to the shoulder inside her ceiling.

"You have a lot of energy," she said warmly, diplomatically.

I settled in a chair and used my hands to brush off my skirt. Ms. Danaan took a file from her drawer. She opened it on top of the ceiling debris.

"The Agency does have several positions for pure flight," Ms. Danaan said, ruffling the papers with her red-tipped fingers. "They are, however, only offered to flyers with great experience and national reputation. You need an entry-level position." She smiled like an aggressive animal, all her teeth showing. "Messenger, perhaps. A fair number of our messengers fly." She looked at the ruined ceiling. "Recreationally, of course."

"Mr. Murdoch referred me," I said, baffled by her words. I showed her the business card he'd given my parents. "Mr. Murdoch's seen my flying, and he guaranteed you would want me."

"Oh, dear, Mr. Murdoch," she said with some grimness. She closed the file. "That explains it. He does these things, I'm afraid. Mr. Murdoch plays jokes on me, and you are one of his little jokes. He retired recently, you know. Sometimes I think I will never be free of his jokes."

I looked at the card. It said:

Mr. Murdoch
Institute-in-Jest
The Agency

Ms. Danaan seemed relieved by the news and less elegantly imposing. She sent me away without a job at all, but before I left she tried to cheer me by reading my palm. It was a hobby, she said, that complemented her work in personnel. She squinted carefully at my hand and rolled it this way and that, assembling the possibilities. Finally she told me that God had granted me three children, two to be a blessing and one to test me.

✤✤✤

"That explains it," my husband said at a much later date. We had this conversation at a time when my shame had taught me to fly only at night. I was not getting enough sleep and my husband was tired of my crossness. "She couldn't give you a job when she knew you would be having kids. How can you fly when there are babies to tend?"

Mr. Murdoch said the same thing.

I was digging then, for a living. I had a selection of shovels and I freelanced holes for shrubs, for gardens, and for pipes needing burial. It was good work, healthy, except when I made the mistake of looking up into the bright daytime sky. I would be overcome with longing.

"You have to sacrifice the children," Mr. Murdoch said when I was working in his yard. Most of my digging jobs came from church referrals.

"They haven't been conceived," I said.

"All the better to do it now," he assured me.

Mr. Murdoch referred me to a necromantic gynecologist who ran fertility clinics. She agreed to cut out the roots of my three unborn children.

I could not sleep on the eve of the operation. To keep from waking my husband, I flew away into the sky, looking for solace but finding only the lighted windows of our church, where I hovered and saw my mother, in gloves and Sunday hat, read aloud the scripture lesson:

> Thou has shown thy people hard things:
> Thou hast made us to drink
> the wine of astonishment.

A clerically garbed Mr. Murdoch administered the wine with a tablespoon, much as my mother had given me medicine when I was a child. The worshipers sat neatly in their pews, braced themselves for it, took the wine by spoonfuls. Each one screwed up his or her face as the liquid coated the inside of each mouth with a phony fruit flavor, a deception that failed to mask a harsh medicinal taste. After the people dutifully swallowed the wine, their eyes opened wide with astonishment as they saw the hard and impersonal truths of the world.

Eagerly I flew inside the church. I took the wine, and my eyes opened. My eyes saw into the past, beyond my mother, all the way back to my grandfather's farm, where a red heifer struggled because her horns were caught in a thicket. Thus Abraham avoided the sacrifice of his son Issac when he found a ram trapped by its horns in the underbrush. He made the exchange with God's blessing. I could do the same.

Immediately I went to the young cow. I thought I would offer her in place of my future children, but God was on her side, had given her a presentiment of this fate and the strength to escape it.

God appears to have a sense of humor very close to Mr. Murdoch's.

Even as I flew to catch her, the red heifer tore free of the brambles and loped away, past my grandfather's gate. Bless her heart, the last time I saw her she was trotting west along the highway, ignoring the airhorns of truckers.

II

In the days when flying became obsolete, I continued to fly and to entertain baseless hopes of glory. My husband tried to dissuade me, but I told him that the loss of my children was as much sacrifice as I could bear. I would not sacrifice my ambition.

He reminded me of our prenuptial agreement to split living expenses fifty-fifty. "As for ambition," he said, "what would you think of the ambition of a fish that longed to walk?"

"I knew it!" I cried, and I became, forever after, suspicious of him. "You are a creationist."

Nevertheless, his pragmatism won. He had me involuntarily enrolled in a human-potential seminar called Reality-Based Living.

Among its participants were compulsive hitchhikers, secret anarchists, women who opened antique shops, honest priests, IRS employees, fashion models, dinner theater actors, and subscribers to *Town & Country* magazine.

The workshop/seminar was a famous, nationally franchised one. We gathered in the largest meeting room of the Hyatt Regency Hotel where we sat in armless stack chairs and held notebooks embossed with the seminar's logo. The three-part plan for learning the secret of maturity was as follows:

> 1. DISCRIMINATE one's dreams from reality.
> 2. SURRENDER those aspects of one's dreams that do not correlate.
> 3. SMILE as one forsakes them.

To my left sat Philomena the hitchhiker, familiar looking, a woman made wise and patient by her intimacy with truckers and with salesmen in Pontiacs.

"The problem with hitchhiking," I told her, "is that it makes you vulnerable to the kindness of strangers. To fly is to escape strangers, to be free of them."

Philomena was very thin. She ate only when someone bought her a meal, and she collected her clothes from the poor bins of Midwestern churches. She gave me a dry and rueful smile. "The hidden vulnerability of flying," she said gently, "is elitism."

I was embarrassed.

I looked to my right where Anthony, the secret anarchist, sat and dripped with sweat. He was having the hardest time, unable to bear the slow and structured pace of the seminar. He gnawed his shirt cuffs. The only meetings he ever attended, he told me, were those of his secret anarchist organization. Their gatherings were irregularly held and never announced—formless meetings during which the non-members, as they called themselves, would sit, stand, gesture, and all talk in loud voices at the same time, each one facing a different direction, each one arriving and leaving at undisclosed intervals.

"When I feel oppressed," I said to him, "I read the Psalms." I told him about drinking the wine of astonishment, and how it opened my eyes to the hard things of the world.

Anthony shrugged. "That's all well and good," he said, tugging at his bit of anarchist beard, "but is it intellectually consistent?"

"Oh, all God aside," I said, "there are some useful scriptures. I can prove it to you."

Anthony looked dubious. At that moment, as if by design, the seminar coordinator (a woman who looked suspiciously like Mr. Murdoch) yelled at me for talking in class.

I laughed out loud. I stood on the plastic chair and waved my embossed notebook. I shouted:

> Ye shall be slain all of you:
> as a bowing wall shall ye be,
> and as a tottering fence.

The female Mr. Murdoch signaled to activate the security system. Rented cops appeared in the corners of the room.

I shouted:

> Let death seize upon them,
> and let them go down
> quick into hell.

Anthony applauded. I continued, thrilled with my own defiance:

> Break their teeth, O God, in their mouth.
> Break out the great teeth
> of the young lions, O Lord.

Drugged and pale expressions filled the faces around me, all but for Philomena. Elegant as a queen disguised in shabby clothes, she stood next to me, on her chair, and she proclaimed:

> Let not them that are mine enemies
> wrongfully rejoice over me.
> Let them be ashamed
> and brought to confusion together
> that rejoice at mine hurt.

The guards circled around behind us. Philomena and I acted as of one mind. We put Anthony between us, we took hold of his arms, and we flew up to the ceiling, then horizontally across it to the double doors, where we ducked down and crashed through. In this same manner we careened down the wide halls, through the lobby, and out the grand foyer of the hotel. Feeling impish, we took a number of hats with us.

Philomena flew like a natural. Anthony was a different case. His thought-filled brain weighed so heavily that when we coached him and let him go for test flights he would plummet straight down, head first. Philomena and I had to catch him by his feet. In this way he lost his shoes and socks. By nightfall he developed a graceless but workable dog-paddle, and the three of us traveled the dark skies, risking collision with birds or accidental decapitation on utility wires. Anthony wore a tie clip that doubled as a penlight, so we used it for illumination.

At daylight we landed, joyful and exhausted, at my house for coffee. My husband pretended not to be annoyed by the unexpected company. He showed us the morning paper, full of stories about a penlight-sized UFO that had been sighted repeatedly over the city and countryside for a hundred miles around.

"You'll never get this flying out of your system," he said, "until you face that there's no money in it."

Anthony shrugged. "There's no money in anything interesting as far as I can tell."

I wanted to prove them wrong. I concocted a good story about the three of us having met and flown with aliens from the UFO. Philomena and Anthony agreed to go along with it.

"If it gets in one paper," I said, "all the other papers will call. We will have speaking engagements on National Public Radio and we can publish a newsletter."

The plan started brilliantly. A reporter and a photographer arrived within twenty minutes of our phone call. They took notes and lots of pictures, during which I levitated, Anthony shouted polemics, and Philomena wore all the hats we had taken from the hotel.

The next week I proudly showed my husband our group photo in a supermarket tabloid. He pointed out to me that there was no article about our aliens. The caption identified us as award-winning vigilantes who had broken up a dognapping ring.

"You look like crackpots," he said.

My eyes filled with tears.

No phone calls came.

We did look like crackpots.

III

I gave up flying.

I sacrificed it, too, rather than endure further humiliation.

To reduce temptation, I nailed shut the bedroom windows and I sewed lead inserts to my shoes. My husband did not dare complain.

I took up, instead, a career.

I joined a pyramid sales scheme and began selling cosmetics

and vitamins at home parties. Anthony recruited me. He showed Philomena and me a wall chart from his anarchist days, an old political theory diagram that he'd converted into a graphic organizer for his sales empire. Arrows and circles expanded in all directions, proving, he said, the profitability of his business.

During my training, Anthony discovered that I had a talent for makeovers, the sleight-of-hand that uses face paint to create from a nondescript woman, her own remarkable and glamorous avatar.

I wanted to practice on Philomena, but she declined. Her only beauty routine was to wash in rainwater. I remade myself instead, redesigned myself so not a blemish, not a pore showed. My confidence grew tough and opaque.

"What of the ethics?" Philomena asked. She followed me, holding the nail jar as I sealed shut the rest of my windows.

"Ethics?" I said. "In selling there are no ethics."

Philomena thought about this. "I suppose I believed the same thing when I worked for The Agency," she said. "Until Mr. Murdoch got me fired. I interviewed you years and years ago. Do you remember?"

I was stunned. I looked at her plain face, naked and vulnerable, like the face of any unimportant person. "You can't be Ms. P. Danaan. She was worldly and successful. She was perfectly groomed. She was older, back then, than you look now."

"I know," said Philomena Danaan. "Isn't it amazing?"

"And you talk to me about ethics," I said bitterly. "Because of you I cut out the roots of my children. Because of you I stopped flying in daylight."

I turned away and banished Philomena from my life.

❁❁❁

After my career's inglorious start (I did not sell a lipstick my first thirteen makeovers) I became enormously successful, hosting six, seven, sometimes ten parties a week, a top producer in my pyramid. I was so grave and earnest that the clusters of women sitting across from me were afraid not to buy my scented depilatories and my vitality-enhancing vitamin powders, my pots of enameled eyelid color and my tonic water for skin.

I remade the women, painted their portraits over the tops of their faces. I understood that they, too, each one of them, had abandoned a cherished hope. Even as I exploited them, I shared their secret grief.

Biological changes happened inside me when I worked. High winds blew; windstorms filled my inner ear. Electric sparks ran across my tongue. My pulse adjusted itself to that of my customer. Euphoria picked me up in a mental state suspiciously like flying.

I made more money than my husband and still I needed to sell. There were not enough home parties to satisfy me. I carried a portable booth to the shopping malls, where I caught women in mid-flight, so to speak, between one store and another, beneath the eye of the security camera. It was tricky to snare customers in the open, like rare and dangerous birds. With experience, I came to recognize the ones who had even a small corner of desire for my wares, and if they had that desire, I sold them.

The ones hardest to stop in public, the ones who conversely most coveted my makeovers, were the haughty suburbanites in their sport clothes. They believed, like a religion, in the makeovers they had already created, and being reminded of the process disturbed them. They believed only the lower classes revealed such intimacies. The well-positioned could not bear to look at me as they hurried through the mall, just as they could not look at janitors and car wash attendants. If one did stop, it was to toy with me, in the mean and naive way of an adolescent on a prank phone call.

Mr. Murdoch, looking prosperous, suburban, and slightly senile, stopped at my booth one day and pretended to want a perfume for his granddaughter. He did not remember me. His manner ridiculed me, as if to say, *Don't you understand the embarrassment of your occupation?*

"But Mr. Murdoch," I said, "don't you think all occupations are an embarrassment?"

Mr. Murdoch used his left hand to stamp his cane on the shining mall floor. His right hand, the business hand, stayed buried in a deep coat pocket. "You don't know my name!" he shouted. "Don't call me by my name because you don't know it."

"But I do," I said, gathering my wits behind the perfect surface of my face. "I am Philomena Danaan. You had me fired from The Agency."

"What agency?" he said.

"The one on your business card," I said, and pulled from my sample case the soiled and tattered card he'd given to my parents eighteen years previously.

Mr. Murdoch looked aghast at the souvenir.

"You are the reason for the ruin of my life," I told him. "You are the one who bedeviled me with pranks at The Agency until you destroyed my reputation, until you reduced me to this, to peddling eye make-up."

"That was a long time ago," Mr. Murdoch said. "I'm an old man now. I'm retired now."

"You will never stop being part of The Agency," I said with authority.

"Surely there is something I can do for you," Mr. Murdoch said slyly, "something you want, something you need."

"Buy out my inventory," I challenged.

He nodded before the lens of the security camera.

"Give up your retirement," I said. "Sell cosmetics and vitamins for me."

He blustered and stamped his cane on the floor.

I thrust out my right hand. "Then it's a deal," I said.

The quickness of my gesture, a lifetime of business etiquette, and the security camera all conspired to trap him. Mr. Murdoch had his own right hand half out of his pocket, his right shoulder jackknifed to his ear, before he realized the consequences of shaking my hand. We stood and looked at one another, me pretending to be in a time warp, Mr. Murdoch struggling with his honor.

I saw that whatever trickery or manipulation befell Mr. Murdoch, it would never be more than what he had administered to others.

With my hand outstretched, I levitated three feet. I loomed over the old man. I repeated slowly and carefully, in the voice of a parent granting one last chance, "Then it's a deal."

He had to reach to shake on it.

IV

I was flying again, or rather, levitating. It expanded my market and my career. Before I learned the secret of enchantment, I sold products only to those who entertained the notion of owning them. Now I had the power to sell to the unsuspecting and unprepared. All I had to do was present my argument and levitate. A helpless, hypnotic glaze clouded the customer until he or she submitted to my will.

Those were heady days.

I sold cosmetic makeovers to the following: a blind, born-again seamstress, a Korean house painter who spoke no English, a homesick Russian spy, the owner of a used-car dealership, a family of migrant workers broken down by the side of the road, a young couple struggling to make their cable TV payments.

I worked one hour a day and wrote twenty-three orders. I was almost rich. I bought a new house for my husband. It had a detached garage for his projects and a spare room so his mother could visit. I bought china and gave our Melmac dishes to the Midwestern poor bins. For the first time in my life, I wore colored underwear and pearl earrings.

I stopped sleeping. I stopped washing my face. Each morning I applied another layer of make-up until it formed a crust on my skin. I lost track of how many days and weeks I had not slept. At night I lay rigid, like the freshly dead, in my bedroom where the windows were nailed shut. Finally, as though I had been waiting for it, a noise came against the glass. Philomena stood outside, tossing gravel at my window.

I met her at the kitchen door. "What do you want?" I asked with the hostility of one who remembers a past humiliation.

"There's something wonderful for you to see," she said, and took my arm.

"I don't fly," I said stiffly.

"The hell you don't," Philomena laughed. She had put on weight and looked more like the imposing Ms. Danaan I remembered, the silver combs back in her hair. Her feet floated several inches above my porch. She carried a jug of wine.

"Maybe this once," I said.

She hurried me up into the night where, in the blink of an eye, the triumphs of my career turned to vapor. We flew like madwomen. We split the wine fifty-fifty, and it inspired us to stunning feats of daring, to stalls and flips and elaborate woven loops.

"Do you see now?" Philomena asked. "Are you beginning to see?"

Due to the wine, I was seeing not one truth, but many.

"There they are," Philomena urged again.

Above us, in the backlit city sky, I saw the red heifer, free at last from the highway. On her back rode my three children.

"Thank you, thank you, Mother," they cried, voiceless, as they slipped away behind the stars. "Thank you for sparing us earthly lives."

They dropped coin-shaped blessings that hit my face like cold round kisses. The blessings washed my skin clean.

"Ungrateful creatures," I said. "They didn't want to be born."

The sacrifices over which I had dedicated such anguish had never been mine to sacrifice at all. In that case, I thought, I would rather fly.

Philomena and I flew, anonymous and spirit-struck, into and around each other until we crash-landed at dawn in the crown of a tree.

"I am finally drunk," I told her. "I am drunk with astonishment."

Letters to Ellen

2/23/71

Dear Ellen,

Of course I will save your letters, but you must agree to keep mine. That way our biographers can work together. They will be a husband-wife team and they will divorce over us. They will quarrel about our significance and become intellectual enemies and wage a custody battle over our papers. Do you want to be responsible for the ruin of their lives? Quick. Destroy my letters. All two of them.

I know in the same time you have sent me fourteen letters. You remind me of it each time you write. That I can count them is proof I have saved them. My Intro Psych class explains this—the letters, not the counting. We are both anal, but I am the constipated sort, nurturing my hard little nuggets of shit, reluctant to let them go, and you are of the diarrheic personality, spewing your crap through a fire hose. Actually, I made that up. I haven't been to Psych class in two weeks. I haven't been to any class in two weeks. It hurts too much to get out of bed. I think my nerve endings have been damaged, burnt away by a sinister gas pumped into our dorm. Lots of girls don't get up in the mornings. February just is not worth living through. I went to the clinic and they gave me yellow pills that make my mouth dry and puffy. How will a dry, puffy mouth help me through February and Intro Psych? I went to the fellow who teaches my section of Art History and she said my concerns are common, blah, blah, blah. She said I sound like an indecisive grad student. That made me feel better. I've always wanted the afflictions of my elders. The problems of my own age are mundane.

I smoke now. I had to learn so I can smoke grass. You will not approve. Neither does my roommate. I have to go next door. There's a rich girl (her father is vice-president of some evil capitalistic corporation) who has a single room that is an absolute pigsty. She must be desperate for friends because her room is available for anything. I go there and smoke and listen to the stereo. I do it as much to escape my roommate who doesn't talk to me anymore. My roommate's a country girl with a boyfriend who wears overalls. She drinks beer like a Viking. She's the only girl on our floor with her own car which makes it bad that we don't get along but we don't and I'm not sure why. I wrote a paper for her on Malcolm X and it got a B-minus. She's gotten locked out of the dorm five times (curfew is eleven-thirty) and I've let her in the back door. Once I let in her hayseed boyfriend and gave them the room while I stayed overnight with the rich girl. I've gone home with both of them, the country girl and the rich girl, and each time I got so drunk I threw up. But I sent thank-you notes. Both sets of parents said they'd never gotten thank-you notes from a college kid.

Two weeks ago Tuesday I missed curfew, and I needed to pull an all-nighter for a paper due Wednesday. My roommate wouldn't let me in and I couldn't wake the rich girl, no matter how much I banged on her window. I'd spent the evening at a group house off campus that's not university students but drifters and hitchhikers and cosmic white-lightning people. They've got aluminum wrap sealed over the windows. The ceiling is draped with Indian bed-spreads. The freezer has more acid than ice cubes. Anybody can sleep there and does but I felt safer walking the streets all night. It was clear and cold so I had to walk fast. My face got numb but the rest of me burned like a furnace. The small-town streets here are wide and dark and empty. There are more stars here than at home. Orion has his usual bold outline, but here there are drifts of stars like veils across him. I felt like I could invent my own myth and fall into the sky beside him and become a new constellation.

At six the library opened. I charged in to do my academic duty. How I thought one writes a paper without a pencil or note-cards I don't know, but I was filled with elation. I pulled out books only to find that in each one, random pages had been cut out with a razor blade. How odd, I thought. Why is it me who sees this kind of thing? Why don't the others notice? Why aren't there school paper editorials ranting against biblio-vandals? I looked in other books and found the same thing. Every one had been mutilated. I opened tens of books and then hundreds of books, leaving them like drop-pings behind me, making a trail of unsteady piles on the floor as I weaved through the silent, early-morning stacks. The books had no endings. From each one had been cut the conclusion and the index and the appendices.

I returned to my room and went to bed and mostly have stayed there. The pills make me sleepy enough to ignore my roommate. I will not end this by asking you to write because you always do.

With love,
Mona

P.S. I don't believe you. How can you read *War and Peace* in one night?

✤✤✤

4/6/73

Dear Ellen,

How unutterably contented I am, blissful and cow-like in the extreme. I feel sorry for anyone in the world who is not pregnant. Perhaps carrying a baby is like spring, sweeter than other seasons because its days are numbered and so brief.

Congratulations on your scholarship. Ten years from now you will be a professor at Bard. You will be published in all the right journals, renowned for your slightly eccentric but level-headed ways, for your astounding insights, all the more breathtaking because they come from a small, modest woman in sensible walking shoes. Am I correct? I have not seen you in two years. Tell me you have not changed. Lifetimes have passed since our last summer together. Civilizations have risen and fallen. Your mother has walked that drooling mutt of yours 1,460 times, a true test of maternal devotion.

Your letters are collecting in our post office box. Please keep sending them. They will be all the more delightful, read at one time, in order, whenever we return to Redlands. Right now we are in Arizona but we have no address. We live in the school bus. Sean and Randy spent the last month working in the copper mine because the engine blew up. Rita and I make hats that we sell sometimes to little stores and sometimes off a card table beside the road. You have never seen such hats, like opium dreams, full of feathers and rhinestones and nylon net veils. I make my own tortillas, patting them hand to hand in a cloud of flour. An old Mexican woman showed me how. We used to be strict vegetarians, all four of us plus Rita's baby, but I learned as we became poor that such habits belong to the bourgeoisie. Dumpster diving is a sport I had to quit because of being pregnant. I have the nose of a bloodhound. I cannot stand the smells. I do double duty as guard and baby-sitter, and when Randy finds an unopened can of corned beef hash, we happily put it in the rice and beans.

Last week I went to the free clinic for a fetal checkup. Sometimes I feel like a Tupperware container with this lively little fish sealed inside of me. She talks to me. I haven't told Randy about her voice because he's getting into weird religious stuff with some Mexicans he met in the mines. If he knew I really hear the baby he'd want me to go get spiritual with their priest or guru or shaman or whatever they call this nasty old man who leads ceremonies out in the desert. I think they kill chickens and dance.

The baby talks to me conversationally. It's the way we live, I imagine, that lets me hear her. We don't have a lot of modern noise in our lives, not even toilets flushing. Think about how often toilets flush in a house where lots of people live. It's noise. Our bus broke down on this road in the desert about two miles outside town. We put up awnings on the north side and we camp under them because the bus gets too hot in the day. We play rummy at night, or we make music.

Until the checkup, and I'll tell you the story, I still had the flute I played in high school. Do you remember how we met, third period band, Mrs. Kneebler, silent K? I used to watch you all puffed up and turning red over your oboe and wonder how anybody could pick such an embarrassing instrument. I don't know an A sharp from a treble clef anymore, but I liked to play music in the desert at night, just these made-up things that Sean calls "Roy Rogers in Utopia." Sean plays guitar and writes songs about the meaninglessness of suburbia. Rita plays harmonica and Jew's harp. Randy is into rhythm. He beats on things. I wish we'd played every night while I still had my flute, but it's hard to get the others to start unless we have a visitor and the guys want to show off how cool they are.

It's so quiet at night under the desert moon, I hear the bubbles when the baby turns inside me. Her name is Nirvana, and she tells me not to seek happiness, that all I long for I already am, I already have. I hold my big happy stomach and her voice links me to the uncountable, faceless, forgotten women with whom I share this sacrifice of my body. I tell Nirvana that, yes, I am at peace, but I cannot stop longing for a daily bath.

I went to the free clinic where the waiting room is wall-to-wall bellies, mostly Mexican girls and traveling hippie girls. The volunteers are good-hearted middle-aged ladies, League-of-Women-Voter type ladies, their children mostly grown and off being successful, the ladies wanting to adopt us girls the way you want to take home the puppies in pet store windows. I found my benefactress filing gray folders in endless metal file drawers. She was so earnest about it. I heard her singing the alphabet song under her breath. I told her about you and your mother, only I said you were my family, and I told her about how Randy could fix anything, even the bus engine he was rebuilding. I told her how the baby Nirvana talked to me, only I said it was in dreams. She took me home for lunch and she let me have a long soak in her tub while she washed my clothes. Then she drove me out to the edge of town and I said I better walk the rest of the way so Rita didn't get jealous. The lady said, OK, she had to hurry anyway to beat her husband home because he didn't like it when she brought down-and-out strangers to the house. He said she was going to get hurt someday doing it.

When I got to the bus it was vacant and abandoned looking, like some deserted refugee camp. After the coolness, the orderliness of the lady's house, our place seemed sinister. "She's gone," Nirvana said, clear as glass. "Rita's gone and taken her baby." Nirvana was right of course. Rita left a note about how she'd gotten her dad to wire her money and for Sean not to go looking for her because by the time he got this message she and little Celestial would be on a Greyhound bus for home. She took all the secret hat-making money we were hiding from the guys, and she took some of the baby clothes I'd been collecting from churches and shelters. That was OK. But, Ellen, she took my flute. It was our last tangible connection, you and me. I am stripped bare of every proof of you. It's this life we lead, possessionless and homeless. I have molted so many times in the past two years that I have, without planning it, lost the souvenirs of my youth. Please send a photo of the two of us. Your mother took scads of them. I will make a shrine for it and Nirvana will grow up praying to you the way some children pray to the Virgin Mary. Are you a virgin still? You never say.

> Yours in remembrance,
> Mona

❖❖❖

7/5/76

Dear Ellen,

Did you go to the Mall for the fireworks? Did your mother go? I saw part of it on the TV news and the press of people looked overwhelming. Do you remember the year your mother took us and that kid she felt sorry for, Katie somebody, to the fireworks, only we went to the Tidal Basin and sat under the cherry trees? There was a woman nearby whose purse got stolen and a bunch of guys chased the thief and it was all so wholesome that we cheered when he got caught. Then the guys beat him bloody.

Erasmus and I got to see our fireworks from the river. My boss took us in a canoe on the Missouri River. His canoe club does this every year. That's such a funny notion to me, being in a canoe *club*, having an official *club* for canoers. I asked him, Steve, my boss, if they had secret passwords and handshakes, but he just looked at me. He doesn't laugh at what I say because I think he thinks everything I say has significance. He's always telling me how meaningful I am. It's funny to be taken seriously by somebody so square. Steve won't tell me his age but he's got to be old, maybe forty, and he wears his hair in long ringlets over his collar and he has a mustache that droops down the sides of his cheeks. He looks just like some historical relative of his in the Civil War. He showed me the picture and it was uncanny how the two of them could have traded places. He's got a wife who's uninteresting, he says, and three kids, although I can't imagine that because he's so uncool with Erasmus, all *ga-ga* over Erasmus like he's the kid of the Japanese emperor.

Erasmus is in the terrible twos now. I told Steve that, and he said, Yeah, just wait. Next there's the horrible threes and then the fucked-up fours and on and on. He didn't seem real optimistic about kids. What can you expect from a guy who doesn't take his own boys to the fireworks? All the other women in the canoes were wives, lots older than me, responsible kinds of women who know how to make potato salad and how to defrost freezers. They helped me show Erasmus how to pee over the side of the canoe. The wives were nice to me in a surprised kind of way. It is because of Erasmus. They are loyal to any woman with a small child.

Erasmus is turning into such an odd little kid. He's glum. He acts like I'm too crazy for the both of us, like I've used up all the craziness he could ever dare be. He eats antibiotics like candy because of his ear infections. I've lost count of the nights Erasmus and I have stayed up because of his ears. We listen to AM radio. You know how when it's after midnight, you can get far away stations that buzz and pop. We do ballroom dancing in the kitchen, just the two of us. We are constant companions. Sometimes I can half-close my eyes and look at his doughy, pouty little face, and I can see his grown-up face, the bones of it, inside him. Sometimes when he has a tantrum he flails and shrieks, all red and sweaty and dangerous like a demon, and I step back from it and just watch. I just observe, and I see how it's his soul he's struggling with. He's mostly a beast, a wild animal snapping at whatever hurts, but inside he's got this nugget of consciousness being born and it's a lot of what hurts. It's his destiny to be human and he fights because it's painful. My grown-up loneliness and confusion pale next to his struggle. Instead I am knocked over by this fierce, demanding love that shoots out of my gut like a projectile. He is part of my soul as much as he is part of my body. Think of that. A part of my soul broke off and enveloped itself in flesh and is going now independently into the world. I can *see* him, Erasmus, as a man, inside the grimy weepy little boy. That's why the scandalized wives are nice to me. They know Steve is a creep and they know I'm a creep for messing around with him. But we mothers have got these little broken-off pieces of soul we're responsible for. We've got that in common and it transcends the other social codes.

Someday I want to go dancing with Erasmus, when he is taller than I am and stronger and more mature. It's easy to see he will grow more mature than I am. Please remind me, Ellen, twenty years from now. You are my memory bank. I forget all these things as soon as the envelope to you is sealed because I trust you completely with my life. You are a better one to hold it than I ever will be.

> With fierce, demanding love,
> Mona

✧✧✧

1/13/83

Dear Ellen,

Merry Christmas! I am instituting a new tradition called the Post-Holiday Greeting. There's a market, I know, among those who do not send cards, who do not participate in the madness and then suffer after it's over. I should have baked turkeys for a shelter and decorated cookies for a children's hospital. I should have gone to a concert of the Messiah and a living nativity at church. I should have gotten my husband something more than drugstore after-shave. I should have wrapped it in gold foil paper instead of the Sunday funnies. I should have put a wreath on the door. Hell, I should have put a thousand lights and an inflatable Santa on the roof. I should have lived. One more Christmas joins the nostalgic past and I forgot to live it. That's what I think even as OP (Other People's) cards invade my mailbox with images of home fires and fruitcake and cute Christmas mice whose lives are more festive than my own. (I notice your card did *not* invade my mailbox. After all these years, have you given up on me? Or have you, too, resigned from the rush? My Post-Holiday Greeting will suit your new lifestyle.)

I forgive you for not sending me a card. Actually, you probably sent one and it boomeranged. In the two years since I last wrote I moved three times officially (meaning the Post Office knows) and twice unofficially. I changed my name twice. In '82 I divorced Dave and took back my maiden name. Three months later I married Jesus Bienvenidos, and in a moment of weakness took his name. I love his name. You would like him, but you would not approve of him. He is from Cuba and has three children by an illegal immigrant from El Salvador. He has a band that plays Latin

Rockabilly, and he works a day job installing burglar alarms for upwardly-mobile yuppies who can't quite afford their new, overly large houses. If Jesus and I get desperate, we know the alarm systems and floor plans for dozens of easily robbable places.

I'm still in sales. I starved during the recession, but things are hot as a firecracker now. I wholesale a tony brand of organic shampoos to beauty shops. We have hair-care products for all the money in your pocketbook. My own hair is short and red. I mousse it straight up. It makes me look excited.

Are you still living with your mom? I told you two years ago you should go back to grad school. You'd love it. You have the perfect situation for it, no rent, no kids, no career. You'd be happy as a pig in mud, reading books all day and debating with aged hippie professors.

My boys are with Dave. I couldn't afford to fight for them, and they're better off with him. They get embarrassed easily, especially Erasmus. He's nine now, and a raving Junior Republican. He called me last week and was talking about trickle-down economics, and I made a crack about voodoo economics. He got all snitty, so I told him his real daddy used to do real voodoo. Well, Dave got on the phone and told me a thing or two not worth repeating. I just don't understand this motherhood business. I thought you were supposed to be genuine with kids. I have never in my life thought two seconds about what comes out of my mouth. But with kids I am expected to write a script before I talk.

Anatole has a birthday tomorrow. He'll be three. He still thinks I'm great. I've got a bunch of gifts for him, but I haven't mailed them. The problem is I shipped the boys their Christmas stuff only last week, so Dave's still mad at me about that. I got Anatole lots of picture books because he loves hearing stories. Kid books are different now. Remember when everyone was white and Mom wore high heels and an apron? Now Mom lives with her butch girlfriend and the kids have suntans. I was at the library last week. I missed the boys so I went to the children's section and sat down and read to any kid that strayed close to me. Most of them got snatched away by stranger-phobic parents, but a few stayed. I read old chestnuts like *Make Way for Ducklings* and *Yertle the Turtle*. The kids brought new books to me, ones with mad, fantastic pictures that make it obvious the illustrators should be arrested for peyote abuse. Instead, they get awards from associations of librarians. They, the illustrators, have learned some secret I never have, about being successful in the world. But I still see things other people don't notice, like how there are no faces in the kid books today. The faces are damp, empty spaces, sometimes with impressions like one might make in clay, but without features.

I saw the same thing at a new beauty shop I'm wooing. It's a very hip shop, done in black, white, chrome, and leather. The head shots they hang on the walls, you know, to show the hair styles, none of them have faces. I made a sales appointment with the manager but she let me slow-cook for an hour while she had a fight on the phone with her boyfriend, so I started going through the fashion magazines with a little pair of nail scissors, cutting out the faces, creating halos of empty hairdos.

Now I will mail this and pray that it reaches you. I think of you often, Ellen, in the way some women carry the daily memory of a lost love. I lie about us. I tell people I went to high school with Chrissie Hynde, that I knew her before she changed her name, before she turned into a chick icon. When I say that, I am really thinking of you. You are my famous person who never got famous. You are the one who deserves it.

> With unrequited love,
> Mona

✤✤✤

3/25/87

Dear Ellen,

I am grieved to hear the sad news about your mother. I liked her the best of all the mothers of anyone I have ever known. She was kind and charitable, and she listened to me blather without laughing at me. She made me feel loved when I was at an unlovable age. How you must miss that love. How I have envied you, living for years with her generous love. What will we do now, without her?

I am crying. I did not expect to. She is an anchor in my memory. She has never aged since the summer of 1970 when I ran away from home and hid in your basement for two weeks before your mother discovered me, although years later we found out that she had known all along. I remember how it was the middle of the night when she pretended to find me. Your dad was asleep. She made English Breakfast tea in a pot that looked like a plum, and we played checkers at the kitchen table. The windows were open. The curtains trembled in the summer air. No one used air conditioning back then. She asked me what I was going to do with my life and I told her I was going to fuck it up, and that is exactly what I have done.

> With sadness,
> Mona

✤✤✤

8/3/94

Dear Ellen,

Jesus killed himself. He was forty years old. He took a plane to Florida. He walked out on the Gulf beach at two in the morning and shot himself.

The turtle people found him. They patrol the beaches looking for sea turtle nests. The turtle people were very kind to me. I had to go identify and claim the body. Anatole went with me. He is fourteen now, and he spends the summers with me. He is a great comfort. He is a loving child, very different from Erasmus, who is at William and Mary.

Anatole and I took a flight into Sarasota. We rented a car and drove to Venice. It is a clean, old-fashioned town on an island. It is filled with vigorous, suntanned, bicycle-riding old people. The turtle people are old. Their faces are full of smile lines and they walk in a busy, successful way. Even on the beach, they walk that way.

Ruth and Homer took us to the place where Jesus killed himself. It was late, after sunset. All evidence of death had been washed away by the ocean. Ruth is a retired biologist and Homer is a retired CPA. They are part of a group trying to save sea turtles by protecting their eggs.

The mother sea turtle crawls onto the beach where she digs a hole and lays one hundred eggs. She cries salt tears from the effort. When she is done, she can barely drag herself back to the ocean. She never sees the babies. All her tremendous maternal sacrifice goes into egg laying. She lays one hundred eggs to insure that one chosen child makes it to adult turtlehood. Only one. The other eggs are dug up and eaten by raccoons. Or they hatch and are devoured by birds of prey during the turtle race for the ocean. Her one precious offspring survives by chance, by winning the lottery of life.

Ruth and Homer want to change the odds. They put wire cages around the nests to keep out coons and foxes and dogs and humans. When the babies hatch, Ruth and Homer escort them to the ocean. Anatole and I got to chaperon the nestlings at the place where Jesus died. That's why the turtle people found Jesus, because they knew the babies were ready to emerge and they checked the site every night.

"Cubans are romantic people," Homer said. "Is this the beach where his family landed?"

I said I thought all the Cubans went through Miami. Jesus' father came to Florida in '51.

"This place meant something to him," Ruth agreed. "Maybe his family lived here awhile. Most of the exiles spent time with menial jobs. Maybe this was where his father did janitor work, or something like that, until he could start his dental practice again."

Jesus and I have lived as such middle-class exiles, that it startled me to think about his dignified father being a janitor, humiliating himself over trash cans and toilet bowls. Jesus cleaned construction trailers once. He said it didn't matter. But he shot himself. I'm glad his parents are dead. They were Catholics, and suicide is a terrible sin. I wonder if Jesus lied about not caring that he was a janitor. I wonder if he died thinking that he was sending himself to hell because he could not bear joining his family in purgatory or seeing his saintly father already crowned in heaven.

"Jesus was romantic," Homer insisted, as though they were friends who had shared confidences. "He shot himself in the heart. Only romantics do that."

The beach where Jesus died is rocky and heaped with sharp-edged, broken shells. The water is green and warm. It rolls on the shore without breaking into waves. Anatole tried to be sad for my sake, but he loved the water at night. He loved the little turtles. They had hatched and were digging out of the sand nest in a frantic group effort. They fit in your palm, and they look prehistoric — ancient, armored beasts, raw with life, unblinking, cold and wet and hard like little stones. The nestlings surged over the brim of their nursery. They swarmed across the sand in a desperate but impersonal quest for the ocean. We guarded them by the white light of the moon. Ruth and Homer let Anatole redirect the lost souls. Normally people are not allowed to touch them. The turtle people do not want to interfere with the instincts that will guide these creatures back home for their own egg laying, but I think Ruth and Homer felt sorry for Anatole. They probably thought he was Jesus' son. Do you know that the first year of life for the sea turtle is a mystery? Once they wash into the Gulf they vanish. Nobody knows where they live, what they eat, how they protect themselves.

I went to the newspaper in Venice. It publishes twice a week. I asked that nothing be printed about Jesus' public suicide. They were agreeable although they had already typeset a small piece. Jesus was a stranger. When the paper came out, I saw on the ninth page a startling, blank, white space, one-and-a-half inches square.

That night on the beach, and two days later on the flight out of Sarasota, I looked westward over the Gulf and tried to see with Jesus' eyes. I could not imagine what he might have seen. His ashes lie in a box. They are indistinguishable from the wood ash in my cold stove, left over from spring. I have forgotten what day that was, most likely in late April, when Jesus built the last fire of the season. When I looked at the placid Gulf, I could imagine only the tiny bodies of baby turtles swimming to save themselves during the lost year of their youth.

Mona

The Close

Karl recruited the woman to sell cookware and knives at the state fairs. No one remembers her name. They began sleeping together in his trailer, mostly because she needed a place to stay. It's not easy to sell the pans, even after scrambling eggs and mashing potatoes in them and stacking them in tiers of five to demonstrate a five-course dinner prepared on one burner. Only one burner worked on the stove in Karl's trailer but they never cooked. He and the woman ate fried foods from the midway, and they sucked coffee day and night.

They pulled the trailer all summer from fair to fair, following the trade. They worked the booth from ten to ten and sometimes to midnight, pacing around each other during the slow times, behind the tables of bunting, in front of the collapsible shelves of silver pots, the black-draped displays of cutlery. When the woman took a break she'd go ride the Ferris wheel. At the top she'd look for the trailer, wherever it was parked at that fair, and she'd think how small and harmless it appeared, like a picture, flat and decorative.

✧✧✧

When a woman feels depressed her vision depresses, so things appear flat. People are flat. When this woman gets weak, and she is selling, her aura turns a vile yellow. Here is how it feels when she is selling. She stands in the booth and hawks the crowd. Long tendrils of color flower from her, but they grow from her pores the way sweat does, and they can sour like sweat does. They billow into the crowd, take form from it, and gradually fall to the ground with the softness of pollen. On days when she is strong, the tendrils are blue and red and they whip out like ribbons in the wind. They flutter across the eyes of the people so the people stop to hear her, and in their eyes she sees the reflection of her snapping ribbons.

֎֎֎

The woman learned to recognize that reflection and she sold to it. Karl didn't believe in the look, which contradicted other things he told her. He used a hard pitch on every prospect.

"It's numbers," he said, "strictly numbers. You pitch ten marks, you make a sale. It works. Don't second guess who's gonna buy and who's not. Stay stupid and play the numbers."

He wanted the woman to stay stupid for sure. He played with the numbers on her commission check. She never told him she knew. Instead of giving her the check that came monthly from the company, he gave her cash. The woman asked him to do that, because she didn't like paper things, written things. But Karl shorted the amount in his favor. He always thought she didn't know much. She wasn't a talker, but she could figure in her head as long as nobody made her write it down.

"We'll work our asses off this summer," Karl liked to say, "and spend winter on the beach."

She had no plans for winter. She used to say that making plans was like trying to run in a dream. You learn not to think about running.

The woman slept with him for the bed. She had a mother back in Maryland but no other family, and she hadn't had a real address in several years. She was a ways past young, getting hefty, long grown into the habit of being stupid, living stupid. Karl didn't win any prizes either, fat all over like fried dough, his lower lip puffed up like a bee had stung it. There were a lot of things Karl didn't know she knew. Karl said she was a natural at sales, as if he was the first one ever told her. He said she played the odds like she owned them. He said she milked the numbers dry as a witch's tit.

The Refrieds worked the numbers too. That was what Karl called the born-againers. They rented booths in the commercial building just like sales people did. One Refried hawked the crowd by giving out fake dollar bills with pictures of Jesus on them. Old women with their middle-aged bachelor sons sat behind plastic models of fetuses. The younger Refrieds walked on stilts or dressed in animal costumes. They put on puppet shows for the children, and they passed out *Jesus Loves School Prayer* buttons.

The best Refried was the one they met at their last fair, near the end of August. Karl and the woman never completed the season. That Refried was an original—the Reverend John Sin, ancient, dwarfish, bandy-legged, his hair unwashed, his second-hand clothes draped over him in every sort of color and pattern until you hardly knew where to look first. He wore, in the blasting heat, a herringbone jacket, a red tartan shirt, a lilac striped tie. He wore plaid pants that some half blind woman must have hemmed up for him.

Their different booths, one of kitchenwares and one of Jesus, faced each other across a concrete aisle. Ventilation fans for the warehouse were broken. The heat afflicted everyone. It lay over the displays like an old she-bear, heavy and smothering and cranky.

"How many units of God you plan to sell, Preacher?" Karl asked the first morning they set up.

The Reverend Sin displayed his Computerized Salvation Test, a piece of unfinished plywood wired with ten toggle switches.

Beside each switch was written a question to be answered yes or no, true or false. The test-taker threw the switches, and a TV screen lit up with what was promised to be a computer analyzed assessment of that person's fate on Judgment Day.

"God keeps track of the numbers, boy," the Reverend said, and he rubbed a bandanna over his knotted face. "I just walk in the places Jesus walked, among the prostitutes and the money-changers." He grinned at the woman and at Karl in turn.

Karl laughed like a hyena. "I showed my troubles once to Jesus, and he told me to take them back, that a sombitch like me deserved them."

The woman had on shorts and a strapless tube top, and she suffered in the heat, her hair wet ringlets of sweat. There were no fair-goers stupid enough to stay in the commercial building. Exhibitors stood idly with each other and bitched about business.

Karl peeled his damp shirt away from his belly. He waved a hand over everything, the Reverend's Judgment Day banner, his own racks of cookware, the acre of tumbled, brightly littered booths around them, all simmering in the jungle air. "Who's worried, Pop? After this, hell's a vacation."

The woman fanned herself with a cookware brochure, wandered across the concrete aisle. She stood before the little preacher's salvation board, slanted like a ramp on top of his card table. Wires joined the board to the old-fashioned TV.

"I want to be saved, Preacher," she said lightly.

Yes. No. She flicked a toggle switch, and a red light burned near it. A string of hand-lettered words ran off beside the light, but the woman rarely paid attention to written things. She didn't read much. It was easier not to. When she was a little girl, her mother had read and read to her for hours, and had talked at her for hours more, but words were like things inside a walled garden. The woman never understood why she couldn't get at the things in the garden.

"Is that bad or good?" she said, pointing to the light.

"It looks grim, baby," Karl said.

The Reverend Sin didn't answer. He looked like an old turtle, his colorless lips pulled tightly over dentures too large for his mouth.

The woman started to read the words, and she recognized them, but the hard feeling in her head made her stop trying, and she pretended to read because she didn't want the preacher to know.

"Answer from the heart, Sister," the Reverend Sin said to her.

She flipped another switch. Heart was all she had. *Yes. No.* The questions had something to do with how a soul got saved. Her flesh spoiled in the heat, turned soft and moist.

She pushed the switches, click, click, click, right and left. The preacher watched her hand like it spelled out a message, like he could read the future in it, like maybe the answer came out differently each time and surprised even him. It thrilled her a little, to be watched like that.

The red lights glinted in a row. The machine hummed. They all looked at the TV.

"Pitchfork City for you, baby," Karl said when the screen filled with red and orange fire. A devil shadow hopped in the corner. "So let's try Plan B."

Karl reset the toggle switches, pushing them upright. The lights winked off and the TV screen turned blank. Karl looked crazy and hot, his skin white glass, the sweat making trembly dewdrops at the tips of his ears. He smelled like a buffalo.

Karl threw the switches again, each one opposite to what the woman had done. She looked on without expression, seemingly without curiosity.

The Computerized Salvation Test results remained the same. The same dancing devil hopped in his corner of flames.

"It's rigged," Karl said. "Preacher, you're a genius. Look at this." He reset the machine, pushed all the switches to *No.* The devil shadow reappeared. Karl pushed the switches to *Yes.* It happened again. "You've got a smartass way to market God. No matter what people say, you get to save them."

The little man grinned so his oversize dentures clicked. "They all need saving, don't you think?"

"They all need to give money to the Reverend John Sin," Karl bellowed. "And they all need my greaseless cookware is what they need." He hollered like he could call to them, wherever they were, the marks, the victims, sick with cotton candy, wandering stupidly over the fairgrounds while he endured the trapped heat of the warehouse.

The woman used a paper napkin to blot the sweat on her face and shoulders. At the far end of the building, workmen on ladders cursed the fans.

"I'm preaching salvation now, Sister, salvation from pots and pans," the little man said as though Karl had never spoken. "Salvation from the hell of this day to the next. You get a new life, Sister, but there can't be nothing of the old life to stand in your way, or it'll block the door and you won't get through. If the eye offends thee, pluck it out. If the hand is evil, chop it off."

Karl hopped across the aisle, braving the heat. He grabbed the ForeverSharp cleaver and handed it to the woman, blade first. "Let's get this salvation on the road," he said.

"Destroy what offends you, Sister," said the Reverend.

The woman shrugged, raised her eyebrows, mockingly sliced the air in front of her throat with the cleaver. "My life offends me."

"You must die," the Reverend John Sin said, "before you are born again."

"Then do the honors, Preacher," Karl said, and he took the cleaver from her and held it toward the little man.

"I sharpen the blade for the one ready to cut," the Reverend said. "I push the one ready to jump."

✧✧✧

What a close. Going for the order it's called, taking the prospect from freezing to boiling, and at the boiling point closing, getting the sale, getting the signature. Here is how the woman feels at the close. She and the prospect are wrapped together in plastic, transparent and airless. They both wait for the other to break, but it's more than that. When she closes successfully she is oval and smooth within. She becomes a mirror, still and clear, so when the prospect looks at her he sees nothing but his own desires. Beneath the mirror she is stroking him, stroking him, hunting blindly for the buttons and springs that loosen his heart, because the sale is made in the heart and seldom in the head. After she closes success-fully she is smeared with her own good fortune, and she doesn't have sense for awhile.

✧✧✧

The workmen fixed the fans. By midafternoon the commercial building got bearable, but people stayed away as if warned by rumor. Karl and the woman didn't write any business. When the exhibits closed at ten that night they went out to the crowded mid-way. They drank a lot of beer and ate french fries. Karl played eight games of Wack-a-Mole. The sugar and grease in the food mixed with their sticky sweat. The midway lights glowered in the hot night air, green and red and blue. The people moved like one beast with many colliding heads.

Karl and the woman went through the fun house. He knew the owner, who had painted it with lewd and primitive drawings of fairy tale characters. Bo-peep's panties showed and Red Riding

Hood wore fishnet stockings. The woman followed Karl up the telescoping stairs and through the rolling tunnel. They got lost in the maze before the tilted room. They stopped at the mirrors and moved back and forth to create their own reflections of coneheads and elephant ears and tiny black spider bodies.

To leave they had to get through the revolving door. It rotated on a platform in a small round room. The woman stepped through the opening and onto the platform. She stopped. She grabbed the center pole and let herself be turned around and around. The room itself was dark, with one window, so as she turned she saw in measured glimpses the colors and faces of the carnival outside. Karl had already hopped into the opposite doorway and he waited for her, but she kept going around and around, passing him by. She felt grown to the place, safe. Then she got dizzy and fell. Still she turned but couldn't get up. Karl just laughed and laughed at her, as if she was as funny as the little preacher.

A couple of teenage girls helped the woman up and off the platform. Karl pretended to act sweet then and took her on the Ferris wheel. When they reached the top he tickled her until she thought she would fall out of the basket.

"It's time to be reborn, honey," Karl yelled. He tickled her bare stomach, under her arms. He snapped her tube top. When the wheel fell forward the woman grabbed the bar so tightly she thought her skin would weld to it. She rose up out of the seat of the Ferris wheel, her center of balance outside it. She plunged forward, into the shining patterns of midway lights.

"Bucking bronco," she heard Karl shout as she regained her balance and thumped back into the seat. "What a sight your butt is, flying in the air!"

"You stop this thing and let me out," the woman yelled to the carny at the switch.

He knew both of them. He laughed and let their basket glide

past him and up again. Karl and the woman completed four circles, all the time wrestling in midair. Finally the carny stopped the wheel. The woman screamed a string of foul names at both men before she ran off alone to the trailer. It probably suited Karl fine because after the midway closed the carnies were having a party in the fun house. Lots of coupling went on there and mean tricks, like anyone who passed out got duct-taped to the floor.

She spent the night looking for where Karl hid his cash. It was in a metal box he had stashed in a space behind the medicine cabinet. She took the big bills, tried twice to count them but lost track at about twelve hundred, sealed them in an envelope with her mother's name and Maryland address on the front. She banged on the other trailer doors until she woke the wife of one of the cotton candy vendors, a surly woman, but quiet. The cotton candy woman had some stamps. She took the letter and promised to mail it in the morning.

✿✿✿

Here is how the woman feels about selling absurdly priced cookware to young brides. She wants redemption from them. She takes their money with a sense of loss because what she really wants from them is their lives. The money's not enough, when they could be telling her how they stand to live from one day to the next and even to appear cheerful doing it, while for her most days are like pleurisy, where the source of living itself causes the most pain.

✿✿✿

Karl woke her at five-thirty the next morning. He came crashing in the door of the trailer and fell on the bed. He smelled of everything foul.

The woman took her clothes and towel and went to the gang shower on the edge of the fairgrounds. Female carnies and farmers' daughters washed up there, in a gray cinderblock building with a corrugated tin roof. The shower room looked bare and hard, a concrete stage, not a stall or a curtain for hiding. Supposedly a lady cleaned. Her Styrofoam cup for tips sat empty on the sink.

Nothing from the world made a sound, except for some quick little brown birds, that seemed to live under the roof. The morning light looked too thin. Heat and the smell of diesel lingered.

The woman showered alone, and she stood a long time in the hard stream of water. After that was when she had her vision of the little preacher. She dried off but left her hair in dripping ropes because it felt cool. Then, naked, towel in hand, she saw the Reverend Sin, only he was the size of a leprechaun and as clever looking, and he sat on the edge of one of the cinderblocks that jutted in from the wall to make a narrow ledge.

"There are false prophets," he warned, "and they ask you to die in the wrong way."

"Dying is dying," she said, and held the towel in front of her.

"Dying is important," the preacher said. "It's the message. Dying is the answer."

"To what?" she asked.

"To rebirth." He breathed noisily, old man breathing that whistled with the sound of the small birds overhead. "It's a brave kind of dying because you have to do it while you are still alive, and it hurts more than the other way which is over, snap!" He snapped his leprechaun fingers.

"I'm afraid," she told the little preacher.

"Then you must find help to do it," he said. "And there is the danger of false prophets."

He snapped again, such a hard snap that he snapped himself right out of existence.

Two carnies walked on slapping rubber thongs into the building. The woman went back to toweling dry while she listened to their gossip about drinking and whoring. They looked twenty years younger than her and hard as iron.

The woman ran the sales booth alone that day. It was busy enough for one. She sold a couple sets of pans and despised both women who bought them. The Reverend John Sin, in the same outfit as the day before, watched her from across the aisle. He didn't look at all like a friendly leprechaun but like the basest of common men. It was one of her nightmare days.

ψψψ

Here is how the woman feels about waking. All days are dreamlike, and when she wakes up in the morning she needs to wake up a second time. She needs a celestial alarm clock to startle her into the second awakening. Her mother used to say never to give up, never to give in, but the woman does so daily, hourly, just to get through the dream.

ψψψ

When Karl hadn't shown up by dusk the inside of her stomach grew cold. She figured he had discovered the theft. She stopped hawking the pans and waited for him. The Reverend crossed their aisle.

"Little Sister," he said, "you are in danger."

"Of what?" she said.

He shook his head. "Sister, there is no mystery. Everything you truly want, you already have."

He patted her hand, and it was such a simple thing. Karl appeared behind him. Was it also a vision? Karl grinned unkindly with his oversize lip and immediately she let out her breath in relief. He did not know. The Reverend John Sin put her hand on Karl's arm and put Karl's hand over hers in what felt like a gesture of ownership. Karl appeared to be in a jovial mood. He suggested they close the booth and go out on the midway again.

The sweet, grease-drenched smell of food and of people was as tangible as the carnival lights. Karl and the woman got on the Ferris wheel and he held her closely. She became afraid then, and knew she had been afraid all along. She knew she could not let go by herself. At the top of the wheel the fair looked muted, flat and harmless. She saw at its outer edge the suburb of trailers. The wheel descended, rolled forward like a dropping bird, swift and unforgiving.

The woman let Karl push her. In the final seconds she grabbed him. The woman wanted him to save her, but she knew he was saving her by letting her go. Even as she blessed him in her heart, she screamed and screamed the entire, unending fall to the ground.

Fly-by-Night Weddings

My mother is a welfare cheat, as am I, for I borrowed three thousand dollars from the credit union for my wedding, knowing that I will give the note to Richard as soon as we marry. Twelve hundred of it I will use to buy my white wedding dress from the Shoppe of Troth, from an exotic entrepreneur who calls herself Madam Vrishna. She likes to wink and to pinch the flesh on my arms. There is no flesh on her, for she is old and thin and lives I think on whiskey fumes.

I found Madam Vrishna through the yellow pages. She has no vanity. She paints her long, untrimmed nails orange, and it calls attention to her arthritic joints. Her face is all bone and colored eyes and rude, clicking mouth. The day I meet her she wears a green caftan fringed in black. Green makes her green eyes shine. Her cheeks are varnished with a cosmetic sexual flush.

Madam Vrishna has wonderful dresses.

"I won't take a dress I wouldn't wear myself," she tells me, "and I've married seven times." Madam's hair is spray-paint black. It looms above her skull like a headdress.

The Shoppe of Troth occupies a dark and narrow storefront, its only decor a wall-size fireplace made of cardboard and painted poorly to represent gray stone, perhaps the hearth of a castle. A disheveled, one-eyed collie sleeps there. When I enter the shop, bells ring, and the dog raises her head.

"A wedding!" Madam Vrishna calls. She claps her dry hands. "How thrilling! A bride!"

Her cigarette smoke hangs in plumes against the ceiling, but her dresses do not smell like tobacco. When I push my face into the fabric, I find the odor of sachet, of rose geranium, lemon verbena, violet and tansy, masking the deeper stink of dry rot and dust. A seam in one linen gown crumbles through my hands like ripped tissue. I tuck it back into the dress rack so Madam will not see.

Like brash parrots strung on a wire, the dresses crush together, shoulder to shoulder, garish enchanted robes thick with embroidered thread, impermanent bright dyes on brocade and wool and muslin. There are no pastels and nothing streamlined. Rich and bulky with detail, hems and trains lie against each other in piles on the floor, lapping wave-like at the rug.

"I am Madam Vrishna," the shopkeeper says, her face that of a wild, old bird. "I will find you the perfect dress."

I hope she will, for I have read three bridal magazines and gone to five wedding stores and have emerged with nothing but the fear that I am an impostor.

"Are you marrying for duty or pleasure?" Madam Vrishna asks.

"For love," I say.

"Duty to him, or to yourself?"

"I said, love."

"Or is the duty to a third party? A crippled mother?"

Oddly, Mother is crippled by her back. She receives a government check with her number on it, and though she and I have read the orange pamphlets we cannot decide if she is cheating. I buy her groceries, pay her electric bill, her phone bill, her cable TV bill, and we don't report it. I'm almost certain the social worker will cut Mother's check if she knows. I don't tell this to Richard. He would turn us in. Although he condones cheating, he cannot abide welfare.

"What do you want to say about this duty?" Madam Vrishna asks, and when I protest she adds, "or about this love? What will you say?"

"It doesn't matter," I tell her. "I'm giving him the bill."

Madam's eyes close, overcome by her wrinkles when she laughs. "And how will you deliver the bill? With a slap?" and she swats my cheek, a touch from which I shrink, "or with a cloying sweetness to baffle him?"

"I want a wedding dress that doesn't look like one," I say, "but it's got to be white."

No lace, no organdy, I think, please, no mother of pearl. No tulle and no eyelet and no milky veil behind which my dark eyes look like twin spiders. As, with increasing fear and desperation I tried at the five previous wedding stores each cream and pastry-batter gown, I wonder what a spectacle they make me look. Hoax is written across my face. I must have failed to grow up because I do not look like a bride. I look like a monkey in a nuptial dress.

When I was small, before my father left us and when Mother still took me to church, I used to draw pictures during the sermon and to write stories on the bulletin. I knew even then that I received a special dispensation for being a child and that I would be expected to change.

My mother changed twice, changed her entire self-image, her values, perhaps even her brain waves and fingerprints. She told me she metamorphosed when I was born. The transition took a three-month postpartum depression during which I was kept by her sister. But when Mother reclaimed me she had faced, she says, and acknowledged her full responsibility. She interpreted life through her motherhood.

The second change incubated for three years during the period of her abandonments. Her husband left, then I did, and finally she lost her health when she shattered her spine and lay riveted to a hospital bed. As soon as she relearned to dial a phone Mother called every social agency in the directory. I read the numbers to her, but she wouldn't let me handle her business. She ordered booklets where more social agencies were listed. Mother has rent relief, tax credits, food stamps, a free wheelchair, hot meals, books for the blind, sample medicines, physical therapy, radical psychiatric counseling, second-hand clothes, and a young lawyer filing for gratis the divorce she'd refused in the past. Mom calls this her retirement. She's done well for twenty-six years of clerking in drug stores and newsstands.

I thought I would change when I graduated from college, and when I didn't, I assumed moving in with Richard would fix me. That was two years ago. I look in the mirror today and see a girl of sixteen, or even ten. She won't die.

Recently, with no apparent motive, I want desperately to be married. Richard does too. We have discovered a swelling, shared devotion for each other in our simultaneous desire. We look at each other with pride.

I do not crave and did not request a diamond, but Richard purchased a large one on credit. He buys me wedding magazines filled with glossy pictures of brides. He gives me a wedding book in which I am to record our joint venture, and a calendar on which he has already annotated the timetable for everything from ordering his mother's corsage to licking the thank-you stamps.

Madam Vrishna disapproves of how Richard is directing things.

"If your groom thinks he can set the mood of your wedding," she says, "you must crush his ideas. The bill is not enough. Men expect bills. You must use a dress so startling, so outrageously amazing that he will learn you won't fit into the little scheme he makes. In fact, he will have to think quickly as you come down the aisle, whether or not he chose wisely to marry you."

"Sounds like I'll need another dress for the divorce," I say.

"I have been divorced also," Madam Vrishna says. "There are other things to tell a man then."

"Are you trying to talk me out of this?"

Madam Vrishna laughs. "Girls cannot be talked out of weddings. It cannot be done."

She finds for me an amazing dress. It would do well as a costume for a miracle play. I consider adding a black silk eye mask and arriving incognito at my wedding.

I buy a dress so white and brilliant it gleams like a beacon in the dimness of Madam's shop. The bodice, sleeves, and hem are trimmed with white fox fur and ribbon and flat pearl buttons. The sleeves are cut in points that brush the floor. They are lined with satin the color of blood and pegged with rows of tiny crystal bells that tinkle in whispers. Fantastic embroidery, white on white, saturates the fabric. Open-winged doves fly between bare dogwood, designs stitched traditionally, Madam Vrishna says, by cloistered nuns.

The train splays behind me six feet. The bodice ends just below my breasts, medieval style, and if I stand swaybacked I look satisfyingly like a pregnant child-bride.

"Should I choose something so white?" I ask.

"Virginity," Madam Vrishna says, "and purity are a state of mind." She lifts the skirt to show me a little pocket sewn in the petticoat and closed with a braided drawstring. Inside is a stoppered vial. "This was for the chicken blood," she says, "in the old days when a bride's wedding sheets were hung from the window. Only a very foolish girl trusts to nature for her stain."

Madam Vrishna does not tell when or where these old days happened, but she speaks as though they are her childhood memories. She chalks the alterations on the dress and I leave it with her. I pay her cash.

ψ·ψ·ψ

When I return the week before my wedding to the dress shop and find it abandoned, I look at the wreckage with the eyes of a dreamer, as one who is filled with wonder but never surprised. I bought my bridal gown while fixed with an enchantment. I believe in the transitory nature of magic.

By pressing my face to the glass of the locked door I can see a pile of wire hangers beneath the empty dress racks, the walls gutted of mirrors and hooks, the rug taken, and torn papers scattered over the linoleum floor. Muddy paw-prints cover the papers. Dust and shabbiness infest the little shop.

I head directly to a parking lot under construction, where I know Richard is working a weekend job in order to pay for my ring. He is directing an asphalt crew, and I find him there in his rubber boots, his funny helmet, enveloped in the stench of petroleum. The father of Richard's college buddy owns the paving company. The father wants to recruit Richard full-time away from the giant construction firm where Richard has just begun working, a rookie straight out of engineering school.

"My wedding dress is gone," I say with false despair. "The shop closed and everything's gone."

Dressed in his overalls and his yellow gloves, with his chin unshaved, Richard is the picture of masculine labor. I want him to take me into his oily arms and say, *Screw it. We'll go to a Justice of the Peace on Monday and get married without the damn dress.* But not Richard. He believes in the Plan of Life.

"Did you go to the right shopping center?" he says first.

"I imagine so," I reply. I am used to this.

"Did you knock at the door? Did you go around to the back door? You should have found out who owns the place."

"No," I say, "I shouldn't. I got what you wanted. I bought the only white dress I can stand, and now I'm not getting married until you find it."

Richard gazes upon me with his well-trained eye. He reads books and takes classes in the power of self and of the directed mind. I love Richard for his absolute certainty in the rightness of himself.

"That's childish," he says.

"You're right," I say. "I'm too young to be married."

"Think positively," Richard says, "think creatively, and you can solve this."

"You're going to solve it. Richard, if I don't have my dress, the one thing I want, the only thing I want out of the whole wedding, then forget it."

"You've tied up your ego in one dress," he says, the reasonable teacher.

"Don't tell me about my ego. Don't tell me what's tied up where."

The shovelers and graders on Richard's crew stop work, lean on the tires of their truck, swill me through their eyes. They measure me for potential fury and Richard for his ability to match it. They all have guns at home, Richard tells me, and they hide the ammunition because their women go crazy without notice.

"And don't start crapping about responsibility," I yell for their benefit. "You're knee-deep in blacktop because you can't pay your bills."

Richard blanches. Just like a tomato dipped in boiling water, his aura splits and peels. "Will you lower your voice? When have I ever let a bill go past due for one hour? When have I failed to meet an obligation? Which one of us is it who forgets, *forgets* to pay bills?"

Then I want to drop it because I am bored. It is a well-worn argument between us, that although I incur few expenses and have few material desires, my bills are paid with penalties on the second or third notice because I lose them among the receipts, clippings, telephone notes, books, used envelopes, tourist brochures, and coupons on my desk.

Richard maintains a rigid, and I think peculiar, punctuality where he meets his obligations by paying the minimum of a five thousand, a ten thousand-dollar credit card bill. He has so many bills he keeps a ledger of them.

"Do you want me to call everyone and cancel it?" I say.

"Iris, we're committed to the wedding."

"I'll not be committed to anything but the state hospital," I say.

"Stop making jokes," Richard says. "You waste creative thinking time to make jokes, and they don't get us anywhere. You shouldn't have gone to a fly-by-night business for your dress. There are reputable places, established places."

"Are you going to find it?" I say. "I did what you wanted. Now you find my dress."

As much as I begrudge Richard his single-minded assertiveness, I am amazed and jealous of it. While I fall into huddled confusion, my fears clogging my brain pores, Richard confronts a problem and solves it. My heart swells with gratefulness when he does this. It's almost a physical rescue.

Within twenty minutes Richard locates by phone the owner of the shopping center, confirms that Madam Vrishna fled that morning after stuffing her dog and her inventory into a cherry red van. The landlord tried to stop Madam Vrishna by blocking her van with his truck, but she called the police and he had to move. There is no law preventing her from removing her merchandise. The landlord tells Richard that Madam Vrishna has another wedding shop in a small city two hundred miles south of us. Richard calls that store and a saleslady tells him it is open.

We drive south in Richard's velour-lined Chrysler, its tire pressure two pounds low for a torpid ride. I feel like a cricket in an ornamental cage when I ride in that car, so I sleep. Richard complains about it even while I'm sleeping, but he won't let me drive.

I dream about my own car, an old Fairlane. It is painted white for my wedding, with lace curtains at the windows. Inside, where the seats used to be, is the bridal bed made up with white linens. I am afraid and upset because the wedding guests can see in through the flimsy curtains, and I know that if I want to marry I must consummate our vows on that bed. The guests stand somber and speechless, twenty deep around my little car.

⚘⚘⚘

Richard wakes me midafternoon as we enter the city. He tracks down the shop with the vigor of a bloodhound after a lost child. The House of Brides is the end store in a small brick shopping center, a dreary, old-fashioned one with missing bricks and fallen rain gutters. There is no back door, but a side entrance opens to an alley, and parked there with its panel open is the cherry red van. The old collie sleeps on a back seat. She doesn't stir.

Lights in the shop are off. The sun casts bright squares inside on the carpet. We try the door, but it is locked. Bells ring when Richard shakes the door in its frame. A tumult of dresses, like heaps of cut flowers, lie on the floor.

Richard taps at the window. "Hello!" he calls, the friendly visitor. "Anybody home?"

"That's her," I say, and I wave and knock and smile.

Madam Vrishna appears momentarily behind a curtain at the back of the store. She looks at us without recognition, her expression fierce. She appears oddly the victim of a head transplant, her face and hair luridly groomed but her narrow body dressed in corduroy pants, penny loafers, and a man's button-down shirt. She stands as erect as a queen.

"Stop her at the side door," Richard yells when she ducks

behind the curtain.

I scud in his wake around the corner, where we find her peeking out the door. Richard grabs it before she can retreat.

"I want a dress!" he hollers.

"Thieves!" Madam screams.

She wins their battle for the door because she has a broom handle she cracks over Richard's wrists. The door slams and we hear the bolt slide shut.

"We have to be reasonable," Richard says. "We have to talk with her."

He runs around front and pounds on the glass. "Madam Vrishna!" he calls. "My fiancée bought a dress from you. We have the receipt." He presses the receipt to the glass and points to it.

The proprietress ignores him. She walks over the dresses on the floor and begins to draw black shades in the windows. There are three shades and a fourth one in the door. Richard runs from window to window, waving his pink receipt.

Madam Vrishna puts her red mouth to the mail slot in the door. "I've never seen you in my life," she says. "I'll call the police."

"I'll call the police," Richard yells. "I'll swear out a warrant for your arrest. I want this dress."

A narrow package falls through the mail slot. When I open it we find two dozen flat white buttons wrapped in a torn piece of what looks like my gown.

"She's mad," Richard says.

"If you'll stop having negative thoughts about her, you can get back my dress," I say. I am most fearful for the rows of crystal bells in the sleeves. I want them for wind chimes. "You can think the dress out of her."

"Don't be smart," Richard says. "It doesn't become you. This whole thinking thing works. I've thought you into doing things differently than you'd planned lots of times."

"I know," I reply. "My mother says don't wish for something too hard because you'll get it. She believes in thoughts. She believes they come true."

"What about it?" Richard says, unimpressed by my undignified mother.

"Don't you ever listen?" I say. "I've told you before. She wished for years she could quit work, and it's come true. She can because she broke her back."

"That's got nothing to do with controlled thinking," Richard says, "or directed energy. I'm sorry about your mom, but she doesn't run her life any more than you do."

I see Madam Vrishna first, on the flat roof of her shop, the false brick front like a battlement that comes to her waist. She is releasing silver balloons that have written on them Shoppe of Troth. From them dangle strings on which are tied my crystal bells. The balloons must be old and left over from some promotion, for they are lopsided and not buoyant. Instead of soaring away they drift out and downward, sweetly ringing like fairies settling to earth. They hover above us and the wind blows the trailing bells. I catch the ones I can. I run around the parking lot chasing silver balloons.

"I told her not to marry you for duty," Madam Vrishna calls.

"You don't even know me," Richard says.

He looks up at her painted face. The wind rises and she throws out streamers of white fabric that flutter and catch and fall in the air.

"She's tearing up my dress," I yell to Richard.

"It's my dress," Madam Vrishna says. "I was married in it seven times." She throws down the blood red linings from the sleeves and ribbons out of the bodice. I have my bells and am satisfied, but now Richard runs across the parking lot, chasing swatches of dress.

"I have a receipt," he yells. "I'll sue you for this."

"You can't sue," Madam Vrishna laughs. "You didn't pay for it.

You have nothing to say about the matter."

"My wife will have plenty to say."

I tear the bells from the balloon strings and wrap them in tissues I find in the glove compartment. I put them in the side pocket of my purse.

"My wife will sue you," Richard says.

"What wife?" I say.

"There's your dress," Richard yells at me. The tails and tatters of soiled fabric spill from his arms like the floppy limbs of some animal he has killed. "There's your dress."

I do not want to look on him coldly, but it must seem that way. I do not feel cold. I only feel separate and apart, like I might have changed in some unrecognized way.

In his rage, Richard begins to cry.

"I'm sorry," I say. And I really am. I give him back the ring and I keep my three thousand dollar note. If this is the first of seven weddings I hope the others are less expensive.

Mary Overton has been writing for twenty-five years but only recently began publishing her stories. She has worked as a low-level government bureaucrat, as a house cleaner, and as a sales rep for encyclopedias, office furniture, and cable TV. Currently she teaches fourth grade in Fairfax County, Virginia, where she lives with her husband and daughter.